MERRY CHRISTMAS, MY VISCOUNT

EMILY WINDSOR

This is a work of fiction. All names, characters, places and incidents are products of the author's imagination. All characters are fictitious and any resemblance to real persons, living or dead, is purely coincidental.

ISBN: 978-1-9161139-4-7

ASIN: B077SRV99X

This book is written using British English spelling.

CONTENTS

LUCKY IN LOVE...

Helmdon Court. Northamptonshire, England. December 16th, 1814.

Asher's indignation deepened.

The damned minx.

A trill of husky laughter forced his gaze from an atrocious deal of cards and to the source of said indignation.

The damned minx. Or more properly named, Mrs Mereworth.

To be truthful, she wasn't the font of his irritation. It was himself. All his life, he'd held the ability to *know* people, to read people. That was his strength, and his weakness. Never did it take long – a few words, a detailed perusal and everything fell into place.

But this slip of a woman sitting diagonally opposite, now serenely chewing on a sugar plum, confounded him.

Indeed, little did she know, as those slender fingers

nonchalantly threw down a winning queen of spades, that she was mystifying one of England's highest-ranked Intelligence Officers, and only one question remained in Asher's mind…

Was Mrs Mereworth a totty-headed innocent or a nimble-witted card sharp?

Everybody had dichotomies, he knew that more than most, but nobody showed such disparity, and it was this fifty-fifty indecision that underpinned his irritation. He did not waver.

Ever.

Disbelief, exasperation and downright bafflement caused him to scowl once more. This simply did not happen to him – newly ennobled Viscount Asher Rainham. Spymaster. Saviour of a prince and a bosky duke.

It wasn't arrogance, purely the truth. Calculation and probability – it all came into play and always gave him an answer. For example, he was ninety-five per cent sure the Marquess of Winterbourne, the minx's partner at this game of whist, would ask her to use his given name before the completion of the current trick.

"Oh, Lord Winterbourne," she purred, "another excellent card. I don't know how you do it."

"'Tis all in the wrist, my dear," replied the dark-haired rogue sat next to him. "And please, call me Jack."

Asher felt some measure of satisfaction that not all his senses were deserting him and waited for her gushing response, but it never came, and narrowing his eyes, he saw the first sign of unease.

Interesting.

Her ice-blue eyes dulled ever so slightly and a delicate hand clenched on her emerald silk shawl, flapping it about.

"Oh, I couldn't possibly. It wouldn't be prope–"

"Come now, Mrs Mereworth," Asher found himself saying, "we are all to be in each other's company for the next week or so, and none of us are young flibberty things."

As soon as the words had left his lips, he cursed his forthright tongue. He didn't mean to imply–

"Speak for yourself," Winterbourne drawled. "Mrs Mereworth is but a beautiful fledgling whilst I am in my absolute prime."

Opening his mouth to make amends, he was forestalled by his own whist partner, Major Lucas Mainwaring. "I believe what Asher was trying to say is that we may forgo some formality this Christmas, as none of us are easily shocked debutantes or tender cubs."

Asher merely nodded. Best to keep his mouth shut before he inserted another large hessian.

He had attended this Christmas gathering at the behest of Lucas – old friend, a damn fine surgeon, formerly one of the best men in Asher's ranks and now the Earl of Helmdon.

Both himself and Winterbourne had arrived at a cosy-looking Helmdon Court yesterday to enjoy two sennights of good company, excellent brandy and the occasional cheroot.

Christmastide, it seemed to Asher, was a fine excuse to overindulge, even if the actual Eve was still eight nights hence, and Lucas's Tudor abode certainly suited the time of year with its blazing fires and plethora of food and wine. There was also no chance of the Prince Regent breathing down one's neck in Northamptonshire. In point of fact, Asher doubted whether their glorious ruler even knew where this county was located.

Prinny had been badgering him to stay in London over Christmas but Asher had suffered enough. This autumn, he'd saved a fuddled duke from a poisoned goblet of wine – French, as coincidence would have it – and had thus been honoured with a Viscountcy...which had cost him one hundred and fifty-nine pounds for the privilege.

Glancing up, he observed Lucas crease his scarred features in contemplation of his cards. Daring and compassionate to a fault, a near-fatal fire in France had left his friend with burns to his face and body. Lucas would also rather be anywhere but here playing whist, as he'd always been mindfully hopeless at sedentary pursuits. Indeed, his gaze kept wandering across the drawing room to his wife Rosalind, eyes habitually drawn to the lady's garish yellow gown like a compass needle to north.

An apologetic brow raised itself as Lucas threw down another fruitless card, but Asher barely shrugged.

They weren't losing due to incompetence, and although he'd like to say the hot punch had impaired his own judgement, he knew it a lie unto himself.

It was her. The irksome, pretty minx.

Logically, he already knew her background – widow, independent, thirtieth year or thereabouts, a previous chaperone and distant relative of Lucas's wife. But he ought to know more.

He glared again, willing her to betray something, reveal anything... But naught, her earlier brief unease now submerged beneath a calm exterior, neither frustration nor enjoyment marring her fair features.

As a rule, Jack Winterbourne tapped his fingers and frowned with impatience when his cards were favourable, and Lucas Mainwaring's leg joggled if his hand was poor – at this very moment, it twitched relentlessly.

Mrs Mereworth displayed nothing except for the occasional raspy giggle at her whist partner's droll remarks, and even that appeared a façade, an affected response.

An hour ago, as they'd sat down to play, he'd been confident of success. His logical brain had always prevailed at cards and he really hadn't envisaged her and Winterbourne as a challenge. She'd fussed with her shawl and fretted at being too near the heat of the fire. Asher had yawned.

When she and her partner had won the first hand, he'd considered it beginner's luck.

During the third, however, he'd begun to think her disconcertingly clever and admired her skill and inscrutable demeanour, but just as he thought he'd twigged her character, she'd proceeded to throw cards down with careless abandon, hardly looking at them, laughing with a gut-stirring huskiness at Winterbourne's ridiculous tale of a highwayman and some mangy hound – a story every lady in London had heard.

So, he'd returned to the luck theory.

He wondered what it would take to rattle that tranquil exterior of hers. What if he reached over and pulled the tight pale-blond curl, currently resting against her left ear? What if he leaned across the exquisite walnut card table, grasped hold of her delicate neck and kissed her?

"Bloody hell."

Hearing Winterbourne snigger, Asher realised he'd cursed aloud and stayed his jaw.

Where the devil had that come from? He didn't dally with women. Hell's teeth, he was lucky if he could remember what to do with them.

Asher glowered at the irksome minx again.

Then it happened.

A smirk. Sudden. And in the blink of an eye it vanished.

But Mrs Mereworth had smirked at him.

He, newly created viscount, the honour bestowed for outstanding services to crown and country, was being played for a fool, damn it.

LILY MEREWORTH swiftly lowered her lashes as those penetrating hazel eyes opposite flashed with something akin to displeasure.

Oh dear, he must have seen her smirk.

Sloppily, she let another card fall to the table. It really was most petty to revel in the annoyance on Lord Rainham's shrewd face but nevertheless, hugely enjoyable.

For the duration of the game, the viscount had glowered, scowled, grimaced and generally appeared quite despondent – all seemingly directed at herself.

A year ago, she would have quailed under the austere stare and disapproving furrow of his brow but no longer.

The new Lily did not quail or look modestly at her slippers. Obviously this nobleman could not stand to see a mere woman best him at whist, so she smiled sweetly and vowed to ignore him for the entire festivities.

Her knee grazed the silk of Lord Winterbourne's breeches and the handsome fellow gave her a lazy, seductive smile as he flicked a jack of hearts to the table.

But honestly, how could one possibly address a peer of the realm by his given name?

It seemed so…so casual, so vulgar. True, she was trying to turn over a new leaf but some modern conducts were beyond the pale.

For nigh on eleven years, she had endured the strict rules of her late husband – decorum, propriety, demureness. His dictates had been ground into her very soul, and although she was trying to ungrind them, they stuck like a stone in one's shoe, niggling and painful.

Lord Winterbourne was a marquess. A lord! She'd choke at using his given name. And besides, should not all peers have superior names like…Reginald or Cosmo or Archibald?

But *Jack*…

"Are you basting the boys at the devil's books, dearest?" A pair of gentle hands descended to Lily's shoulders. "I'd be careful, gentlemen. She is a whipster in silk."

"Don't give away all my secrets," Lily replied, swivelling to be blinded by her distant cousin's buttercup satin gown. "And what's a whipster? I thought it a man that drives coaches."

Lady Rosalind Helmdon merely smiled. "I'm actually here to steal my husband away. The babe is deafening our nursemaid, and Lucas is the only one able to calm her. I think it's his raspy voice."

The husband in question stood only too keenly, knocking the delicate table, and Lily wondered at the whole story being no more than a ruse.

"I'm sure no one will miss me," he lamented rather too heavily. "In fact, I think Asher has been playing on his own for the last half hour."

"Oh, less than a quarter, I'm sure…not that I was counting."

The two men smiled warmly at each other and Lily wondered at their obvious bond as she couldn't imagine the brawny and amicable Lucas being friends with such a disapproving curmudgeon.

Lord Rainham's teeth had gritted as she'd laughed, bringing forth memories of her late husband and his critical ways, so she'd giggled even louder until the viscount's jaw had looked ready to snap.

"Well, I've had enough of winning," declared Lord Winterbourne as their hosts departed for the nursery. "What say you, Mrs Mereworth, to a glass of champagne?"

"Thank you. I believe that would be most refreshing… my lord."

Smiling, he sauntered off, and she cursed her inability to be less proper.

After all, it was quite probably this handsome marquess who would be assisting her with the completion of number eight on her list of bold new life resolutions, and there were only so many days remaining until her self-imposed deadline of Christmas Eve.

Begun a year ago, this list had served to focus her determination – to be the 'new Lily' or perhaps the old one that she had lost during her marriage.

Even after her husband had met his untimely end, she had continued to live as though under his gaze. Her very identity had been lost… Mrs Mereworth was purely a replica of that deceased gentleman but with a different title.

But that replica was fading; she no longer wished to be the prim Mrs Mereworth. Instead, with Rosalind's help, she was striving to rediscover her younger self – bold and happy. To have the confidence to laugh and speak freely without censure or grave scrutiny.

She would now strive to be…Lily.

Last November, she had begun her bold list by burning a book – a wicked thing to do, one might say – but *Miss Pikesworth's Guide to Etiquette* had ruled her life for so long that she'd felt trapped within its well-thumbed pages.

Since then she had accomplished six other resolutions

and yet two bothersome entries remained. The fact that these bothersome two were originally Rosalind's ideas was perhaps not a coincidence – the lady had always been a bad influence with her sinful suggestions for Lily's more reticent self.

Still, she had agreed to them, even signing her name at the bottom of the list with a confident swish. Surely these last two could be achieved at a Christmas gathering?

But that oh-so difficult number eight worried her.

She'd ignored it thus far, pretending it wasn't there. Always letting her eyes slide over Rosalind's fiendish contribution...at the very bottom of her list.

Over the past year, she'd thought it might've transpired by chance.

It hadn't.

Perchance the list might've become wet, number eight erasing itself.

But no.

If anything, it now loomed larger and bolder than ever before. Three words that struck such trepidation...but also a most unladylike thrill.

Seduce a rogue.

But was seduction even possible if one couldn't bring oneself to use a nobleman's given name? After all, "Oh, Lord Winterbourne" would be far too protracted to sigh in passion...purely as an example.

"Where did you learn to play whist, Mrs Mereworth?"

Her eyes flitted to the questioner. Lord Rainham. He lolled back in his chair, seemingly relaxed, but she noted his tightly clasped hands and piercing gaze.

When the viscount had first arrived at this house, he'd been a consideration for the fulfilment of resolution number eight.

Handsome with a whipcord body, he appealed to her physically, so different from the late Mr Mereworth's blond, soft looks. A slight grey stippled this viscount's chocolate-brown hair, betraying his age to be twoscore or thereabouts, and although he appeared weary, it did nothing to detract from his sheer masculinity.

Pity he was such a judgemental dull dog, but when in London, she had found many nobles to be somewhat elitist.

"My father taught me," she eventually admitted, although he hadn't pressed for an answer, despite her long pause.

"An excellent teacher, if I may say, and an even more intelligent pupil."

Lily clenched her shawl tight, despite the roaring fire.

After all those irritated glances and scowls whenever she'd picked up a winning trick, was he being sardonic? The top-lofty prig.

"Have you something against intelligent women, my lord?"

WHAT THE DEVIL?

Asher was at a loss. For some reason, he'd upset the lady. Was it the age comment? He really hadn't meant it that way, but it had been some while since he'd conducted small talk with a female. And she *was* comely.

"Not at all," he replied honestly. "I admire intelligence in all species of animal." Wincing, he realised he could have phrased that better.

"Animal?" she growled, sharp blue eyes glaring as she leaned forward and poked his arm with the tip of her finger. "Are you now calling intelligent women beasts?"

"Confound it, we are all beasts under God's sky, Mrs Mereworth. Men and women." He clasped the wrist that fed the poking and slender bones moved beneath his firm grip. "Are you always this prickly? 'Tis akin to conversing with a hedgehog." The pad of his thumb brushed unbidden over her pulse – it beat fast and strong.

"And do you always liken people to animals?"

Asher released her wrist as though burned. "A hedgehog, Mrs Mereworth, would not be pertinent enough. A fretful porcupine would be more fitting."

She stood, and etiquette forced him to his own feet. He remembered that at least.

"In which case, my lord, you are a patronising goat." Mrs Mereworth whirled, a rustle of silk as she stalked off in the direction of Lord Winterbourne and the champagne.

"A goat?" he muttered to himself.

How belittling.

NINE OUT OF TEN CATS PREFER JACK

"Lord Rainham reminds me of my late husband. Judgemental and disapproving. He lures you in with his good looks and firm...jaw. But it's all a hoax. The viscount obviously dislikes clever females. Beasts indeed!"

Standing in the wood-beamed sitting room, Lily folded a babe's blanket, making sure the corners exactly met, and placed it next to Rosalind's hopelessly crumpled attempt.

Lost in thought, she nearly picked it up for refolding but then remembered – no one in this house cared if the linens were misaligned; it simply didn't matter. Instead, she smoothed a hand over the soft cotton, inhaling the scent of roses.

"You think Asher Rainham is handsome then?" Rosalind asked, haphazardly shoving another blanket together.

Lily took herself to perch on the edge of the chaise, narrowing her eyes, back straight. "It wouldn't matter if he resembled Lord Byron. Are you matchmaking, Rosalind?"

No answer came, merely a pursing of the lips, which was worrying.

Before Rosalind's marriage a year ago, Lily had been her chaperone and although they were both intensely private people, she had not failed to pick up on the fact that Rosalind had a unique talent for being insightful.

"Anyhow," Lily said firmly, "I much prefer Lord Winterbourne's easy company." *But could you call him Jack,* an inner voice questioned…to which she feigned deafness.

"Hmm. Asher asked him along to our little gathering as the marquess had a few widows on his tail in London."

Lily's cousin, so many times removed they'd lost count, collapsed on the chaise next to her, legs lolling. Forever, Lily had envied Rosalind's loose style and natural ways but although she had tried to copy the younger girl's manner in line with her new life resolutions, it always felt peculiar and false.

"Is that supposed to dissuade me from Lord Winterbourne? And how well do you know Lord Rainham? If you call him…Asher."

The word almost stuck in her throat. She and her husband had only used their given names in bed and even then, after having addressed him as Mr Mereworth all day, she had sometimes forgotten.

Rosalind huddled up, her cold hands sneaking into Lily's shawl. The icy weather had arrived early this year to freeze one's bones, and certainly, it felt as though winter never really left England these days. Just as flowers were at their peak, the cold began once again, the nights grew dark, and the pretty-coloured petals leached their hue and faded from memory.

Sleet had fallen whilst they'd played cards yesterday, the frosty damp penetrating the old Tudor manor despite the many warming fires, and this morning a thin layer of ice encased the scenery. Pretty to look upon but hazardous.

"If I tell you something, you must keep it secret," Rosalind whispered, budging close. "Asher was Lucas's superior."

"You mean… Oh."

So much could be deduced from those whispered words. She knew Lucas's former occupations: Major. Reconnaissance Officer. Spy.

But she also knew that some years ago, Lucas's superior had saved his life in hideously dangerous circumstances. Which also meant that Lord Rainham was not merely some handsome, disdainful, aristocratic fribble of a viscount. He was Lucas's gallant and courageous rescuer, and last night…

Oh, dear heavens. She'd called him a goat.

"That doesn't alter my thinking," she said, clearing her throat. "You should have seen his face every time I won a trick. He was furious and kept glaring at me."

"Lily, having been on the end of your winning ways, I *can* sympathise with the man. You are a mathematical genius and combined with your…impassive demeanour, he may have simply been frustrated."

"Hmm. I will observe his behaviour at dinner," she vowed, deciding to change the subject. "And when can I see your new babe and her brother? The little one was asleep when I visited the nursery."

"No doubt we will have the chance to play with Alice later but considering she awoke at five this morning, 'tis not surprising she's worn herself out. But Robert…" Rosalind picked at a thread on the armrest. "He is with the males of the house assisting the tenants. It helps if he is…

active. We still haven't found a suitable tutor for him, although at eight years old, it is a pressing matter."

Lily patted her hand.

After seven months of marriage, Rosalind and Lucas had decided to adopt a one-year-old babe from a London orphanage this summer. However, as they'd been about to step from the door with their precious cargo, a young boy had thrown himself at their knees, beating their legs and evading a large guard.

Eventually, it had transpired that this boy was the girl's older brother, but the orphanage, worried a troublesome lad would prevent the adoption, had hidden him away.

"Is he calming down?" Lily asked tentatively.

Needless to say, Lucas and Rosalind had taken in the boy as well, shocked the orphanage would consider splitting a family, especially as Robert had cared for little Alice on the backstreets of Whitechapel for five months, filching handkerchiefs to pay for a wet-nurse after their mother had died.

Rosalind sighed heavily, tucking a stray auburn lock of hair behind her ear. "Not really. He seems so full of anger for one so young. He fights with the village lads and still believes he is unwanted, although I don't know why as Lucas dotes on him, teaching him to shin trees and catch slow-worms. I found one in the bed yesterday – I'm not sure if it was Lucas's or Robert's doing, but I christened the slimy thing George."

Lily frowned. "My husband's given name was George."

"I know, Lily dear." Grinning, Rosalind stood and stretched. "I may nap before the high jinks of the children tonight…and I'm not speaking of Alice or Robert. We have three more houseguests arriving and quite a few neighbours attending for the evening."

"Have you planned all the entertainments for the coming days and nights? I can hel–"

Rosalind waved a hand. "I have the days organised, although it depends on the snow."

"Snow?" Lily held a finger to her chin, gazing out at the thawing ice under a cold but utterly clear blue sky.

"Hmm. But the nights… Let's just say, you will *all* be involved. I'll announce my plans at dinner."

That sounded ominous, but Lily refrained from asking. Rosalind could be as mute as a fish when she wanted.

"By the way," Rosalind said from the doorway, poppy-red skirts twirling, "have you completed your list of bold new resolutions yet?"

"Erm, I have only two items outstanding."

"Excellent. Well done, Lily. And will you be able to complete them before Christmas, do you think?"

"Erm." She tried to picture Lord Winterbo– *Jack's* face, but a pair of hazel eyes matched with a strong jaw got in the way. "One's best laid plans can always go awry, but I hope so."

"Wonderful. Your bed chamber is on the corner. Very private." And with that Rosalind shot into the hallway, leaving mice the only audience to Lily's sharp intake of breath.

Despite the cold, she reached for her silk fan. Coming up with this bold list last year had been all very well, but now the reality of accomplishing number eight scared her rigid.

Number one had been a doddle, burning Miss Pikesworth's book on etiquette – or Miss Pukesworthy as Rosalind now called her.

The late Mr Mereworth had gifted it to her on the occasion of her nineteenth birthday, and he'd even underlined pertinent quotes and added advice in the margins. At the time, married so young and so in love, she had sought to follow all the rules, but it had never been enough.

She had never been enough.

Attempting to sprawl on the chaise as Rosalind had done, she realised it gave her back ache and so sat up straight again. Perhaps one couldn't teach an old dog new tricks.

The second resolution had been to read a salacious novel, and last December, having found an entire shelf of them in the library of the Earl of Stonebridge, another distant cousin, she'd sat down to read and not been heard of again until St Stephen's Day.

Her husband, even when young, had never once disrobed for their marital consummation, so she'd found the novels most enlightening.

Indeed, Mr Mereworth had considered denuding oneself rather common, for the lower classes, and she hadn't known any different. So they'd struggled with billowing nightshirts and frilly rails, and although she'd felt desire, it had always been repressed by decorum and yards of material.

One sketch from *those* books, which always caused a minor flush to break over her body, was of a lady sat atop a male.

Completely naked.

Could she do that? Did she want to? She tried to imagine Lord Winterbourne in such a pose, but failed miserably. He was too...urbane and might laugh at her awkwardness.

Swiftly, she banished the vision.

Another immediate aim for the year had been financial

independence, and so her third resolution to visit a gaming hell had seemed a legitimate solution.

It had all been a resounding success. Lucas had come along, his size keeping the bucks and rakes at bay, but eventually the owner of the hell, a dull little place, had asked her to leave – she'd quite emptied his pockets.

In order to never be reliant again, the fourth resolution had been to invest said winnings together with her meagre savings. The Earl of Stonebridge, him of the well-stocked library, had lent his man of affairs and after studying all the options, she'd instructed him to invest in shipping and perfumed soap.

Every day, she now studied business journals, newspapers and forecasts, moving money around and investing in new projects. She was good at it, and to her surprise, no one had been…surprised – they'd instead asked for advice.

Her income now allowed for luxurious satin and frivolous ribbons, and she'd even thrown away all those cumbersome cotton night-rails and bought half a dozen diaphanous silk fripperies; she'd be found one winter's night frozen in her bed but at least she'd look elegant.

Then there was unresolved number five, a Rosalind contribution: imbibe exotic new-fangled absinthe.

In London, she'd tried to find the strange green beverage, but none of the balls or routs had served it. As a matter of fact, many had never heard of the drink, and what with the war, French tastes were hardly in favour although she'd heard the formula was originally Swiss. Lily put a finger to her lip. This would require additional thought.

A Mayfair ball had provided the opportunity to achieve further resolutions on the list: stay out until two in the morning and waltz with a libertine. Mr Mereworth had lectured that late nights caused one to drop crockery, when in fact it had aided her sleep, and the libertine had been fine-looking but denser than a plum pudding, so not a candidate for resolving the devilishly difficult number eight.

Hmm, yes, number eight.

Originally Rosalind's suggestion had read 'Seduce the first bachelor that the Earl of Stonebridge invited over', but Mr Hagden had been fourscore at least…with no teeth and a teetering gait.

And so the proposal had been amended to allow for a little leeway. Now it merely stated 'Seduce a rogue'.

Merely?

How?

By what means did one go about it? Were there signs one put out? How could one tell a rogue? And did it matter anyway?

Weren't all men, to some variance, rogues?

She'd met Mr Mereworth at a dinner occasion. A handsome man, she'd been overwhelmed by his keen attention, not even considering his personality or the fact that he'd told her she was using the wrong knife. At eighteen, she'd thought him kind-hearted and educated, and they'd married after a whirlwind courtship.

Mutton-headed nincompoop.

Last year, each one of these resolutions had seemed exciting, adventurous, and everything she remembered being as a young girl. Everything she had always wanted to be as a woman.

Pondering, Lily rose and wandered to the door. Which to resolve first?

Absinthe or seduction?

❄

WINTERBOURNE COUGHED LIGHTLY, lined up his cue and scored a winning hazard with the target red ball into the corner pocket.

"Good shot," Asher commented, his back to the fire, a drained glass of brandy in one hand. How agreeable this Christmas gathering was turning out to be. "Perhaps I should have selected you as a marksman."

Surveying Winterbourne play billiards presented Asher with another side to the complex marquess.

Most only saw a sociable, amusing rake, but Asher had kept an eye on him for quite a while and appreciated his ethics, adaptability and affable seriousness – another dichotomy, but there it was.

This past spring, Asher had approached him to work in the Intelligence Service. Men liked his attitude and women liked him full stop. Very useful.

"Too solitary an occupation for me, I'm afraid," Winterbourne responded after scoring another two points. "Prefer the information-gathering side of things. I like talking to people, hearing their stories, making them laugh...and divulge."

"Is that what you were doing with Mrs Mereworth last night?"

An eyebrow raised itself over the cue. "Interested, are we?"

"Bloody hell, no."

A second eyebrow lifted.

Maybe he'd been a tad overenthusiastic with the "no". But he wasn't interested, just...curious.

Realising Winterbourne would be some while at the table, Asher sat himself in the comfy leather chair and poured another drink. They'd agreed that whoever scored would remain in play, but it appeared he'd been hoodwinked – obviously Winterbourne was still wreaking revenge for the codename Asher had assigned him.

The Games Room felt warmer than other areas of the old house, probably due to its smaller size yet huge fireplace, which wouldn't have looked out of place in a castle. Decanters dotted the side table, brimming with amber liquids, and a pack of cards lay carelessly strewn over the round table as though players had moments ago left the room.

Yes, this is what he'd come for: conversation, excellent brandy and to lose at billiards. Not for beguiling, insulting, devilishly clever women with husky giggles.

"She is, without doubt, enchanting," said Jack, chalking his leather-tipped cue, "but delicate."

Asher spluttered his brandy.

"Delic– Do we have the same person? She called me a goat last night and poked me with her fingernail. I'd have thought a widow like that would be your ideal conquest."

"A luscious temptation, but I think not," Winterbourne said, shaking his head and allowing his black locks to fall neatly into place. "She is not a woman for a light dalliance. She would want a man's heart and I don't believe I have one. I mean, it's there, thumping away, but it lacks depth, I'm afraid."

Not believing him for a moment, Asher said the first thing that came to mind. "She is a mathematical minx with nerves of iron. I can usually sum people up very well."

Potting Asher's own damn ball for another two points, Winterbourne laughed. "And I understand women…so perhaps she is a mystifying mixture of both. You like her then?"

"I might admit her laugh is enticing and her skill at cards fascinating. But I once carried out a study of myself and assessed it likely that ninety-nine out of a hundred women would detest me after a day of solely my company."

The marquess chuckled again as though Asher was joking – he wished he were.

Unfortunately, a knowledge of others' faults and weaknesses meant he could also analyse his own – he was pedantic, boring, worked long hours and, unlike Winterbourne, didn't know one single story about a mangy cur to make a woman laugh.

Oh, he wasn't entirely without charm. He could plagiarise another's words and repeat trite phrases but deep down he was exactly what his family had dubbed him: the odd one out.

"I think," Winterbourne said, sighting another pot, "you may be surprised. You listen to people. And sometimes that is the most important thing one can do for another."

His cue ball whacked the red, which careered across the table, missed the pocket and bounced off the cushion. Asher rose in relief and reached for his cue, until he noticed it hurtling back down to hit his own white. That ball then slowly rolled inextricably towards the middle pocket, sliding in with a clunk.

The comfy chair enveloped his backside once more and he took another sip. He hadn't learned to play this gentleman's game until his mid-twenties so his skills were pitiful, and it was a shame Lucas wasn't here, as they had roughly the same level of incompetence, but he'd taken his adopted boy Robert to the village. The lad had got into fisticuffs with a tenant's son whilst out today and Lucas was parleying a truce.

Bit like the peace treaty with France – both resentful,

both probably lying and both masterminding the next battle.

“Well,” Winterbourne proffered, “if you need any wooing advice, just ask. I did a fantastic job for Kelmarsh.”

Asher choked again. The Earl of Kelmarsh had retired from his ranks in May for wedded bliss and was at this very moment rusticating on his estate. Asher had once asked Kelmarsh what love felt like and he’d replied he felt lost and incomplete without his now wife. How puzzling.

“At his retirement spree,” Asher reminded crack shot Winterbourne, “he said you’d been as useless as an empty bottle.”

“He’s happily married, isn’t he? Damned ungrateful fellow. I don’t know why I bother. Oh yes, I do. It’s seeing the agony on their faces turn to smiles.”

“And you say you haven’t a heart.”

“Faugh! And you say there isn’t a woman for you, but remember one thing, Rainham,” he said, pushing the score slider to its furthest mark, “you may have calculated that ninety-nine women may not be able to stand your company, but you’re only looking for the one.”

DELEGATION – THE SECRET TO A SUCCESSFUL CHRISTMAS GATHERING

"Welcome, guests and neighbours alike to Helmdon Court. Myself and Lady Helmdon sincerely hope you all enjoy this early Christmas feast."

Depending on the state of inebriation, hurrahs or polite applause rang around the dining room. The first course had only recently been served, having been delayed for the vicar's arrival, and so pre-drinks had been consumed on empty stomachs resulting in all-round joviality.

As Lily demurely applauded Lucas's greeting, she couldn't help her gaze from stretching across the table. Lord Rainham scowled at the silver cutlery and then started to rearrange it – in width order – aligning it against the serviette.

Endearing, but she had to bite her lip to stop from saying how hopelessly out of sequence it now was.

She'd sat down to dinner tonight without prejudice towards the viscount. After all, Lily's marriage had shown her own judgement to be woefully lacking, and as Rosalind had suggested, it was possible those scowling glances during the card game had simply been frustration.

Alas, she'd always found it difficult to read people, although both Mr Mereworth and Miss Pikesworth had advocated discreetly lowered eyes at all times, so perhaps she hadn't been looking properly.

A variety of invitees were celebrating with them this Saturday night: neighbours from the locale and three further guests from London, one of which sat to her left. Introduced as Viscount Reginald Stretton, he had arrived with his sister who was friendly with their hosts.

Dark with a Byronesque ruffle to his hair, Lord Stretton was quite a good-looking gentleman and had a number of prerequisites for the fulfilment of number eight: good teeth, sweet breath and thin lips.

Mentally, Lily added him to her list of potential candidates, although for some reason only in pencil.

Maybe his hands were the problem. They reminded her of Mr Mereworth's – slightly short and thick, as though they had stopped growing too soon, white and soft. His fingernails also appeared over-long and the image of them stroking her skin produced a cold perspiration.

Her unbidden gaze snooped across the table again.

Lord Rainham retrieved the soup spoon from his tangle of cutlery. Agile, graceful fingers clutched at the handle, although she noticed a nasty burn scar along his palm. Dark hairs sprinkled the back, skin tanned against the white of his unfussy cuff.

Something not altogether unpleasant curled in her stomach, so she shifted focus to her left and met Lord Winterbourne's amused gaze.

"And how are you tonight, my enchanting Mrs Mereworth?"

Really, how could she consider anyone else for the attainment of number eight but Lord Winterbourne?

Stylish and handsome, she should venture to be more at ease with him, so she took a sip of soup for courage.

"Please, call me" – the soup and word got stuck – "Lily."

Immediately, she sensed, rather than saw, her dinner companions stare.

Lord Stretton opened his thin lips first. "Lily? Sounds like it belongs to an opera danc–"

"What a delightful name," a firm voice interrupted, and she looked up to discover that hazel gaze contemplating her.

Such striking eyes and she found herself transfixed.

"Indeed," added Lord Winterbourne, "a flower of beauty and purity – it suits you. And I would be honoured to address you as such. But I say again, you *must* call me Jack. And I'm sure Rainham over there would be only too delighted to hear his given name on your lips, hmm?"

She frowned at *Jack's* teasing glance and turned to Lord Rainham. "Ash… Asher." As soon as the word was released, she noticed his pupils widen, a green tint flashing in the autumn brown before he raised his glass and thanked her.

As the servants cleared the bowls and busied themselves with presenting the next course, Rosalind stood and tapped her champagne glass with a fork to gain the table's attention – not a simple endeavour as those at the more disorderly end of the table, which included the vicar, were intently conversing upon the merits of boar or goose for Christmas dinner.

Lord Stretton's eyes widened, a sneer appearing, as Rosalind resorted to clanking the champagne bucket instead, which certainly did have the desired effect.

Once, she too would have scoffed at Rosalind's lack of etiquette, possibly even given her five pages of Miss

Pikesworth to read, but now she strove to recognise different virtues: kindness, openness, love.

Lily began erasing Stretton's name from her list.

"Now, everybody, pin back your wattles." Their hostess grinned as the table quietened. "I have decided that each of our house guests must host a night of entertainment."

The neighbours cheered. The house guests looked fretful. Lucas groaned.

Rosalind didn't need lists to be bold, her slenderness belying a spine of iron…bordering on brazen.

But Lily felt trepidation stir deep within.

"What kind of nightly entertainment?" drawled Jack, eyebrow raised. "Hunt the pillow?"

"Innocent pastimes only, Lord Winterbourne." Rosalind wagged a finger. "But I leave the choice to you. Games, charades, music, books and so forth."

Another groan emanated from her husband.

"No shirking," she continued. "There are prizes for the winner of each event, and I have already drawn lots to allocate you each a night. Lord Stretton, I must apologise as your name was drawn for tomorrow, which I hope gives you enough time, but please feel free to use the footmen and ask for whatever else you require."

"When is your evening, my love?" Lucas enquired.

"Mine was last night and cards," she retorted smugly. "Lily won as usual and will receive a bottle of something for her triumph."

"Charlatan," slurred the vicar, who seemed to have caught up admirably after his late arrival.

Rosalind merely sat, smiled sweetly and told them all to still their chops and eat their partridge.

"I'm not bloody well organising anything," Lord Stretton pronounced whilst scoffing potatoes. "My title goes back to Stuart times, unlike some upstart tag-rag and bobtails who are given it for sneezing," he said, disdainfully glaring at Lord Rainham. "My peerage was presented by the King himself on the battlefield. I do not organise *games.* Mrs Mereworth, you will coordinate for me."

"I don't think…" she began.

"No, you don't need to," Stretton declared, smothering his peas with gravy. "I will think of the entertainment and you can organise it." He glared with beady grey eyes, as flat and colourless as fog, a chubby white finger pointing. "Have you any ideas for your own night?"

"I don't really…" Her words faded as she recalled such a dinner party with her husband. He'd asked what music she'd arranged, but faced by that pointed finger and harsh tone, her mind had gone blank and she'd felt so stupid.

The feeling returned – a rising cold of foolishness – and she said the first thing that came to mind. "Snapdragon, I suppose," she whispered. "It's normally for children but it might be fun an–"

"Capital idea," Stretton bellowed. "I'll do snapdragon tomorrow night. A man's game – fire and brandy. You stick to needlework and sherry."

"But…" She clutched her shawl tight against the numbness that encircled her.

ASHER WAITED for the spirited and beautifully named Lily to put that mouthy ignoramus in his place.

And waited.

Where was the minx from last night who'd called him a goat?

She shrank lower into her chair as loudmouth shouted

over her, ordered her about and then stole her idea. Asher couldn't bear it any longer.

"I believe, Stretton, that was Lily's idea, for her to use, should she so wish. Do you wish, Lily?"

He paused as she worried her lip, but loudmouth started up again. "She doesn–"

"Enough, Stretton," Asher warned. "We are waiting for a lady to speak and should she not desire to reply until the Last Judgement, we, as *ennobled* gentlemen, will patiently anticipate her words until she deigns to state her requirements." He softened his gaze on Lily. "Take your time. I haven't even begun on my partridge."

"Thank you...Asher," she breathed.

The succulent morsel of meat stuck in his throat. The way she spoke his name slid like a caress down his back and landed somewhere unmentionable.

"I believe, Lord Stretton," she finally said, "that you may keep my idea of snapdragon, as I'm sure I will think of another." The scurvy scaramouch opened his mouth again, but Lily's voice firmed. "I will also not be organising your entertainment. I am at this Christmas gathering to enjoy the company, not to have demands placed upon me."

With each word, the lady became the bold minx of the night before and the icy look she turned on Stretton made Asher's gut quiver. His own family had always called him peculiar and maybe there *was* something innately wrong with him if a scornful blue gaze aroused his more primitive instincts.

ASHER SAT with Lucas's mother on the ample sofa, appreciating the general glow of merriment that filled the drawing room. Dinner had been...insightful and pleasant, and now everyone sat replete, listening to the music or chattering.

Helmdon Court appeared such a cosy place, putting his own bleak townhouse to shame. He enjoyed the long hours at work, but maybe he'd relish being at home more if it had some curtains.

Winterbourne played the piano with panache whilst Lily turned the pages, giggling as the rogue flashed his ivories.

A sudden pall overcame Asher.

Never had he felt particularly lonely, content with his own company and the diligent work he produced, but watching this joyful Christmas gathering, he wondered if he'd missed out on something.

"And how did you celebrate Christmas last year, my lord?" Lucas's mother asked. "As a young girl, I remember much revelry, but lately methinks it to be out of fashion."

"I passed the day calculating the risk of ice breaking on the Thames if another Frost Fair took place. Fifty-four per cent, although I didn't plan for the elephant. That would have added another twenty."

It was bad luck really that Winterbourne had stopped playing at that very moment and rotten timing that the conversation had lulled just as he'd opened his mouth. But all those coincidences had happened, and he found himself the subject of amused glances and smothered mirth.

It didn't matter when he made such dull statistical utterances at the office – it put pompous aristocrats in their place, but at a Christmas gathering…

A saviour in pale blue floated over. "I heard that a pig sailed down the river on a slab of ice from Westminster to Blackfriars Bridge, squealing all the way. Is this true? I know of no one that can verify the story."

"It is," Asher replied, smiling. "The pig was rescued, I hasten to add."

Guests laughed and began to regale their own tales, reminiscing over the ice casino that had graced old Father Thames, and Asher's feeling of oddness seeped away in the good-humoured atmosphere.

Lucas's mother winked and stood, allowing Lily to take her place on the sofa.

"Thank you," Asher said. "I'm not so adept at social chatter."

Her lips curved. "And thank you for rescuing me from Stretton. An obnoxious man."

"I was surprised you didn't call him a goat or some such."

A dimple appeared in her cheek and all of a sudden, an overwhelming urge to kiss her entered his head. Perhaps he was coming down with a brain fever. It was devilishly cold out.

She gazed up coyly. "Yes, I… I believe I must apologise for that. I thought you indignant last night…at losing."

Asher smiled. "I admit 'twas a novel experience, but I was not indignant at you, but rather myself. A…rarity entered my thinking and I miscalculated the odds."

"Do you always reason with probability? Lucas mentioned you work in the Foreign Office. Diplomacy and whatnot?"

Whatnot indeed. Asher wondered how much she knew of Lucas's previous profession, as with that astute mind, it wouldn't take her long to work out Asher's place in things.

"I do. And I'm not prone to taking risks, hence whenever a judgement must be made, I weigh it up, factor in actions, and then come out with a probability of likelihood. If it's below sixty per cent, I *never* do it."

Even when carrying out assignments as a tracker, years back, Asher had always been methodical. Most men in his profession worked on instinct not probability – one chap had sworn by an itchy neck, but then he was dead, itchy neck snapped by a turncoat.

"Never?" Lily asked.

"Nev–" He halted as Lucas's laugh bellowed out, his scarred cheek pulling into a wicked smile as Rosalind whispered something in his ear. *Never* wasn't quite true, he realised. "Only the once, actually, some years ago now. There'd been a twenty per cent chance of success," he finally answered.

"And did you succeed? Was it worth it? Despite the low odds."

He watched Lucas drop his lips to his wife's neck, a flush heating her cheeks as a hand caught her waist, a wealth of love in their gaze.

"Yes. It was worth it," he murmured, remembering the state of Lucas as he'd pulled him from the burning wreck of a chateau-prison in France.

Asher's own superiors had told him to leave Lucas there, saying there was no hope for the man once he'd been imprisoned, but then it hadn't been their orders that had got Lucas captured in the first place.

And so Asher had assembled a small loyal company of men and gone off alone: forty per cent chance of finding Lucas alive.

They'd been awaiting their opportunity, when the chateau had been set alight by other prisoners, the cold night sky lit up like hell itself: thirty per cent chance.

Asher had battled through the smoke, flames licking the sodden clothes that he'd dipped in the river: twenty-five per cent.

He'd found Lucas, scarcely breathing, fallen at the bottom of a collapsed and burning staircase, and dragged him out into the night, rolling him over in the ice-cold grass: twenty per cent chance of getting him back to English soil alive.

Lucas abruptly looked up as though hearing Asher's vivid thoughts and gave a rakish wink.

A soft touch on Asher's hand reminded him he wasn't alone.

"How did you get this burn?" Lily asked, brushing her fingers along a scar to his palm.

"A fire in France."

"Asher Rainham, you are a very..." He waited for the word 'odd' that always followed. "...rare man."

Twisting, he stared at Lily Mereworth, those ungloved fingers still brushing his hand, and her keen eyes, burning as winter's frost, blinked back.

Her coiffure had slightly wilted in the heat of the room and a curl hung precariously, held by a single pin. Her hair was long, he realised. No false wig pieces or weird stuffing but all glorious, pale-blond, glossy locks.

What would it look like freed? Falling in limp coils over naked shoulders, a superb deal of cards held in delicate fingers, sky-blue eyes glowing with intelligence and longing.

A rush of something peculiar gripped him.

Was it...desire?

Desire for Mrs Lily Mereworth?

The damned minx.

WITH HIS BLUE AND LAPPING TONGUE, MANY OF YOU WILL BE STUNG. SNIP! SNAP! DRAGON!

"Put the bowl over there." Stretton pointed. "No, you imbecile! On the other table. Devil take it, I'll have you dismissed for brainlessness."

Rosalind leaned close to Lily on the chaise after shaking her head and smiling at the beleaguered footman. "Do you think if I stick a pin in Stretton, he'll burst?"

Indeed, Lily thought, with his flapping mouth and bulging eyes, he resembled a stuffed toad about to erupt, and he wasn't even a vague consideration for resolving number eight any more – maybe her judgement had improved with time. "Why did you invite him?"

"Came on the coattails of his sister Catherine. She's a delightful girl, if utterly downtrodden. Haven't you spoken with her yet?"

"I tried at church today, but Lord Stretton glares and she backs away."

"Poor dear. She's in love with Sir John Buckland but her brother won't allow a union."

"Don't tell me, he's also invited."

"You know me so well," Rosalind answered, eyes

twinkling. "You talked with Jack a lot today. Is he your favourite? After last night, I thought Asher may be the chosen one. You did sit with him for quite a while."

Lily fiddled with the tassels on her shawl and gulped sherry, gazing around the room to avoid Rosalind's knowing eye…and question.

Awaiting Lord Stretton's evening entertainment were twelve or so guests milling about the drawing room. Fewer than their hosts had expected as Lucas's distant, and apparently tedious, family and heir had got stuck in the mud somewhere in Staffordshire.

Still, a merry gathering and Lily was enjoying herself immensely. They had listened to a splendid sermon by Vicar Daniels this morning and then pots of tea had followed at the vicarage. She'd sat next to a few local farmers; it had all been so…informal.

Playing with the children had rushed this afternoon along until an early dinner. And yes, she had conversed with Jack a lot, because late last night, whilst in bed, she'd realised something.

Lord Rainham, as she was now back to calling him, was dangerous.

Not bodily, of course, but rather she sensed he was not a man for a light dalliance or quick affair. She'd misunderstood him during the card game but last night…

The way his eyes had pierced her, the questions he had asked, interested and incisive, the way he had attentively listened to her replies, the manner in which he'd defended her – it all served to make her wary.

From Rosalind's divulgences, Asher's own words and the burn scar on his agile hands, she could be quite sure he was the valiant man who'd saved Lucas from near death.

That type of man would want more.

He could quite possibly filch a woman's heart without her ever being aware. That woman would simply wake up one day and discover Lord Rainham had stolen it with his protective ways and kind intelligence, his strong fingers and slightly odd mannerisms.

And Lily wasn't prepared to let her heart go rambling off ever again.

"Jack is the ideal candidate to resolve pesky number eight," she finally admitted to Rosalind. "Rainham is too… erm. Well, Jack is younger and…"

Forest-green eyes blinked. "True, stamina is important. You should choose the specimen with most staying power."

"Stayi– Rosalind! I didn't mean…" But Rosalind abruptly stood and smiled her apologies as her adopted son Robert wandered in, looking petulant.

Sipping more sherry, Lily watched as the large bowl on the table was filled with brandy by the harassed footman until Lucas came to sit next to her, his colossal body swallowing the entire space.

"Rosalind's been here, hasn't she? I can smell roses."

Lily tried not to sigh at the romanticism of knowing another's scent so well. Her heart may not go toddling off any more but it did appreciate the sentiment.

Groaning, Lucas swiftly sat bolt upright. "Hellfire, Stretton's using my best bloody brandy for this event. Doesn't he know all the alcohol gets burned off? Damn lackwit."

"Your evening's entertainment is tomorrow, is it not, Lucas? Have you thought of anything yet?"

He buried his head in large hands, messing up his shaggy blond mane. "No, and I spent all night wracking my noggin. Came up with nothing."

Lucas raised his head, a man desperate. "Don't suppose

you've had any more dazzling ideas? Snapdragon was inspired. I would have kept it and told Stretton to rattle off and jump in the lake – the lower one, it's bigger." At Lily's shake of the head, he merely sighed, a man defeated. "By the way, your present for winning cards is in the library. A clue – it's green, strong and needs a lot of sweetening."

"Have you found me a wild man of the woods?"

A smirk twisted his lips. "Absinthe, dear Lily. I cadged a bottle from a club in London."

"Oh, thank you," she said, clasping his arm. "I know exactly what to do for my night of entertainment on Thursday."

Indeed, the unresolved number five on her list had suddenly become so much easier and she could have hugged him – but that would be awfully inappropriate.

"At least someone knows what they are doing," he groused.

A RAT. No, too nice, Asher quite liked their inquisitive nature.

A bull was apt, but far too generous to the man's rutting capabilities.

Maybe he should venture into the vegetable kingdom.

Yes, without doubt, Stretton resembled a turnip – useless, bland, always got too big, and then required pulling up and disposing of.

Asher sat back, quite pleased with his analysis, even as he acknowledged it was gravely immature. But then Christmas was a time for the child in everybody…he'd heard said.

The men in his ranks had all been designated codenames, and he'd followed his own mentor's tradition of using animals. Most fellows delighted in their sobriquet, although occasionally it wasn't quite what they were expecting. People oft saw only the limitations whereas he valued the subtleties, the strengths in all creatures.

His analytical gaze rested on Lily.

Lily…

In some ways, she still confounded him. Shy yet bold. Intelligent but reticent. Cold yet fiery. He would have to give her further consideration.

Winterbourne had replaced Lucas on the chaise beside her, like the ubiquitous moth to the flame. Asher told himself he didn't mind as there was no place for a woman in his life, but her husky laugh abruptly filled the drawing room, hitting his gizzards…and other places he didn't care to think of.

The turnip clapped his hands to garner everyone's attention, and all except himself complied with the demand.

A FOOTMAN BEGAN DOUSING the candles and Jack rose, offering his hand. Lily considered it a fine hand with tapered fingers, short neat nails and a ruby signet ring glinting on the smallest finger, but it somehow lacked…roughness.

"I believe," he said, looking distinctly devilish in the darkening room, "the revelry is about to commence."

Lily took his arm and together they approached the table.

When young, she had played snapdragon with her parents and brother, but after her mother had died from fever, a gloom had descended upon the household, never to lift. Her father had turned sour and critical, always finding fault, and her brother had only too readily left for a life at sea. No more games had been played.

Guests huddled around with obvious excitement. Lord Stretton made a big fuss of sprinkling raisins and nuts into the bowl of brandy and tried to order everybody into a queue, but no one took any notice, instead edging closer.

All appeared ready, and the last candles were extinguished, the only light now being a faint glow from the hallway. Someone bustled past, knocking her into Jack, whose arm slid around her waist for support. He didn't remove it and she couldn't help but wonder why she felt…nothing.

Shouldn't there be a slight shudder of pleasure? A quivering of the lip? Didn't the heroines in those wicked books she'd read last Christmas always feel a clenching of the belly?

With a long taper, the warmed brandy was lit, whooshing up in blue flame. The guests startled, silenced by the sudden violent nature of fire and alcohol as it danced in the earthenware bowl, swaying and daring them to steal its stash of confection.

Everyone peered at each other across the table, faces caught in the uncanny blue glow like demons in a frozen hell. Jack's eyes grew harsh in this dissolute light, not benign or affable but sombre and tormented. Opposite, Rosalind stared into the flames, her features ethereal and entrancing.

Stretton grinned smugly at the onlookers, seemingly pleased with *his* choice of entertainment.

Looming at the back like some dark angel was Lord Rainham. He took one step forward, eyes scanning the crowd and bowl of fire, until fixing his gaze upon her.

A ripple of something…odd and her breath faltered.

All of Lord Rainham's weariness had been erased in this eerie light, betraying a tense and alert demeanour. His whipcord frame stood firm, and she wondered what it would feel like to have all that power and strength unleashed. Those strong hands wandering over her naked skin with determination and intensity, his–

"If everyone doesn't hurry up," Rosalind chided, "the alcohol will burn off and Lucas's best brandy will all go to waste."

The fun began.

Billy, another lad taken under Lucas's wing, plunged his lanky fingers into the burning liquid and then quickly snatched up some nuts, stuffing them into his mouth, obviously an old master at snapdragon.

Young Robert stepped up to the challenge, Lucas hovering behind with a hand to the boy's shoulder.

"Quickness is the key, Robert," he said, but the lad shrugged off his touch, shoving fingers into the glowing flame. Lucas held his breath, arm outstretched, but Robert hastily withdrew, blowing on his heated but empty hand.

"Want to see how a dragon does it?" teased Jack, and they all gawked as he merrily stabbed into the spectral flame and retrieved some raisins still alight.

Lily watched amazed as he thrust them into his mouth, blue flame clinging to the sweets, and as he laughed, it danced over his lips – a dragon in truth, breathing fire.

Once the audience had gasped at such daring deeds, his mouth closed, dousing the blaze.

"Ouch," he promptly said.

Laughing, others stepped forward to outdo one another but burned fingers and spilled raisins resulted, sticky liquid everywhere. Stretton's sister amazed them all, quick and nimble, and even Lucas's mother managed to snatch a nut.

Lily was surprised to see Lord Rainham stride to the table, dark gaze transfixed on the flare of fire, his movement into the bowl so rapid it defied the eye. Had those fingers even touched the flame?

"I have a..." He squinted disappointedly at the item in his palm. "A gold button?"

"You gain a boon instead," Lucas explained. "Anything you want."

"Anything?" he repeated, and Lily gulped as she felt the full weight of his stare. Did he mean–

The flame faltered, beginning to wane, as even Lucas's best brandy couldn't sustain for too long, and so in keeping with her new bold self, Lily swiftly took her chance.

But her assault on the raisin was too slow and she snatched her fingers back with a yelp.

"Over-dawdling, Lily, my dear," admonished Jack. "Why don't you cool them down outside."

Taking her singed fingers to the terrace, she breathed in the fresh pure air, a welcome respite for her lungs and skin alike. She stared out but only darkness peered back.

"Did the dragon burn you?" A deep voice murmured, and she spun.

Hands rose to her shoulders, steadying, and a lustful shudder ran through her.

Drat.

But at least her lip hadn't quivered, and her stomach was definitely behaving itself.

"It did. Too slow, I suppose. I don't know how you managed it, Lord Rainham." There. Saying his full name placed...distance. Made her intentions known.

The gentleman merely smiled, and she could have

sworn that rather than just removing his hands, they slightly slid, slightly slipped, lingered even.

Or was it her imagination?

Or wishful thinking?

"You should cool your skin on the marble of that bench."

Taking his advice, she lowered herself to sit, pressing scorched fingers to icy stone.

"It's cold," she complained. As were other parts of her lower person. "My nurse always swore by butter for burns."

Lord Rainham also sat before covering her hand with his, and glancing up, she became only too aware of how close they were. She could smell lemon and brandy, pungent and fresh.

Still his hand encased hers, but it wasn't at rest. It rubbed, the sensation making her lip tremb–

She bit her lip. It had not trembled, of that she was adamant. And even if it had, it'd most probably been the glacial weather.

"The cold is better for burns, I've found."

"Is that how Lucas survived?"

His brow folded a little. "Ah, you know about that then?" At her nod, he continued, "I believe so, yes, and it is becoming a better-known treatment within medical circles."

Lord Rainham interlaced his fingers with hers. The marble warmed.

"Did you enjoy snapdragon?" she asked. "What have you claimed as your boon?" She'd noted his disappearance soon after his button prowess.

"My boon has been granted."

She didn't dare ask.

"But I do prefer games with more intelligence involved." He grimaced. "That makes me sound a dull dog, and I do not mind watching others have fun. I just don't always...understand it."

Lily pondered. Did she favour daredevil Jack with his dragon tricks? Was Lord Rainham a dreary stick-in-the-mud?

Withdrawing her hand from that firm grip, his rough skin abraded, and she cursed the fish she'd had for supper as her stomach did a slight flip. "Does that make me a frivolous cat then for enjoying this game?"

Lanterns adorned the terrace, a flickering radiance gently swaying and throwing his face into harsh relief. He didn't look dull or dreary, but potent, and so–

"No, not at all. In that blue flame, I saw you as more of a...phoenix."

Lily stilled. A phoenix. She liked that, a revitalised creature of fire, from...ash. "How very flattering," she finally said, noticing he was leaning closer and that her body was also curving forward.

"I never embellish to flatter," he said, their white breaths mingling in a prelude.

He was going to kiss her, and she was going to let him. The snapdragon's fire had nothing on Asher Rainham, as every single part of her felt ignited, and she hadn't even dipped fingers into those flames yet.

Whilst the night hushed, he tilted his head and purposeful lips came so near she could feel the warmth of his skin, taste the brandy. Her eyes fluttered shut.

"No! I got more raisins, so I should win."

Lily's eyes snapped open.

Lord Rainham stood, glowering at the open door. She

must look a perfect pigwidgeon leaning forward with such a pitiful expression.

Quiet but resolute, Rosalind's voice concluded the raisin debate. "Jack won, Lord Stretton. It wasn't the quantity but the technique."

"I…erm," Lily mumbled, and straightening, she rose, stumbled past Lord Rainham and ran inside as though a dragon were truly on her tail.

SOMETIMES THE BEST IDEAS ARE LAST-MINUTE ONES

A bacon aroma pervaded the breakfast room, but the scent of desperation was stronger. Lucas crunched toast with a desultory air and Asher could only concur.

Last night, he'd called Lily a phoenix. How utterly irrational.

It wasn't even real but a fabled creature. And what about admitting to only liking games of intelligence? What a crosspatch he must have sounded. And then, as if that wasn't enough, he'd tried to kiss her whilst sitting on a frozen marble bench. No wonder she'd run off like a duchess caught in Seven Dials.

He steepled fingers under his jaw, a classic pose that always made his men tremble in their boots, imagining him disappointed or angry. In reality, he adopted this affectation when unsure about something, but no one knew that.

"What's wrong, Asher?"

Well, no one but Lucas. He unsteepled his fingers.

"Just mulling over my entertainment choice. I have to

find something for Christmas Eve, which is quite daunting."

"At least you've got four days to ponder." Lucas peered at the mantel clock. "I have nine hours."

"Still not thought of anything?"

"No," his friend grouched. "I considered taking everyone down to the village inn, but Sir John thought of it too, and Rosalind is keeping a closely guarded list of guest's ideas now, so there's no filching."

"Can she not help you in any way?"

"Told me that's cheating. I even complimented her puce walking dress this morning to no avail."

Asher buttered another piece of toast and cut it into equal quarters. "What about blind man's bluff?"

"Nope. Taken by Lady Sidlow for the twenty-seventh. I believe she wants to grab a handful of Winterbour–"

"The bridge of sighs?"

"Nope. Our vicar, would you believe, suggested that one. He's staying for a few days next week."

"Hmm, there must be something."

They both sat back, sipping coffee, content in each other's silence. The ladies of the house were making ready to descend on the village in preparation for the upcoming St Thomas's Day and so the men were being left to their own devices.

A ride over the estate was on the agenda. Maybe an exhausting gallop would eradicate thoughts of Mrs Lily Mereworth, as every time he closed his eyes, he saw either Winterbourne's arm clasp around her during snapdragon or her lashes drift shut as he himself leaned towards her.

Lily wasn't a flirt by any means. In truth, she seemed unaware of her own attractiveness, but she did flitter between them somewhat.

Biting into the square corner of toast, he wondered why he was taking such an interest anyhow. A day spent with him and she'd soon become exasperated at his mannerisms.

And what was it about her? He had intelligent, skilled women in his ranks but never had he felt such a visceral desire to be near them and certainly never to kiss them.

"How's the family?"

Asher choked on his crust. "I saw my elder brother a month ago. He's fine. In service of the Earl of Dunway now."

"Hmm. I saw the earl at Tattersalls last month – horrendous jacket. Was that your brother's doing?"

"I don't think so. Lewis does try and talk him out of violet, but the man has too much money and too little taste."

Asher helped himself to more coffee, hoping to wash away the bitter taste of his family. He loved them and they... Well, he thought they loved him back, but it had always been from a guarded distance.

They hadn't understood where his ambition had come from. Hadn't understood why he didn't want to follow in the age-old family profession of valet service.

Nobles from across England clamoured for a Rainham as valet, their discretion and taste admired by all. And yet Asher, despite his aptitude for precision, had never been able to tie a cravat to any semblance of perfection.

Day after day, he'd sat back and admired his father's skill at false flattery and neckcloths alike, but when a fourteen-year-old Asher had attempted those same disciplines, he'd ended up with reams of creased material and a disgruntled marquess.

A mere quirk of fate had resulted in Asher being

employed as third valet to Lord Sandcroft, an astute gentleman and high up within the Foreign Office. He'd soon discovered Asher's more curious talents.

"You could have invited them here," Lucas offered, and Asher shook off his stale thoughts.

"Thank you. But they..." What could he say? They'd probably scorn Lucas, believing all noblemen to be idle wastrels, ignoring the fact he'd served eons of time in the army, before ending up with a bullet in the leg and scars for his trouble.

The men of Asher's family may be valets but they'd always seen themselves as superior to their employers – perhaps that was why the masochistic aristocrats liked them so much.

This past autumn, Asher had invited two of his brothers to the new townhouse, but they'd belittled his taste in books and asked why all his coats were black. Nothing had changed. They seemed to think it had all landed in his lap, not grasping the hours he worked or the danger he'd encountered in the past.

Perhaps if their mother had lived longer, it would have been different. She'd loved them all equally, never giving favour. A washerwoman, her love had been boundless, indifferent to class, money or intelligence. Despite only being able to write her name, her innate wisdom and essential kindness had outclassed them all.

"No need to explain, Asher. We can't choose family, only our friends. And sometimes," Lucas continued over a maid's angry hiss from the hall, "we can't even choose our friends. Do come in, Stretton, and leave the maids alone."

Striding, the turnip made for the sausages and then plonked himself at the table. "Nothing wrong with a bit of morning fun," he said sulkily.

Lucas aimed a glare. "If you so much as lay a finger, you'll be sleeping in the snow. Rosalind says it'll be falling soon."

"Pah! There's no sign of snow. Your wife must be bird-witted."

The turnip slunk back in his seat as Lucas narrowed his eyes – an intimidating display with his breadth, but the scars added a certain *je ne sais quoi*…and the pointed meat knife aided. "If my wife said it was going to snow frogs, then you would do well to heed her words."

That very same wife bustled in followed by Lily, and Asher couldn't subdue the gratifying feeling that twisted inside his chest at the sight. She wore a pale-blue cloak that matched her eyes, a small same-coloured bonnet perched precariously upon a carefully arranged head of curls, and a pink rosy glow suffused her cheeks – she looked ravishing.

"We are off to the village. What are you men doing?" Rosalind asked, leaning down to her husband and curving a hand around his nape. Lucas arched to her loving touch and Asher yanked his gaze away from their tenderness, his eyes colliding with Lily's, who was obviously doing the same.

The colour of her attire caused those glacial depths to shine and he couldn't quite believe he hadn't been able to read her during the card game – she was now unsure and skittish at seeing him.

She licked her lips and he smiled. Had she wanted him to kiss her last night? The thought sent a shaft of arousal careering through his body.

"Good morning, my enchanting ladies!" Winterbourne's dulcet tones interrupted their gaze, and she turned with a pleased expression and profuse greeting. A low growl emerged from Asher's throat, causing Lucas to look up, eyebrow raised.

Asher coughed, and the eyebrow lowered.

"Exercising the horses, I think," Lucas eventually replied once his wife had removed her hand. "But if the weather turns, we'll play billiards or somesuch."

"Doubt you army types are much good at the gentleman's game of billiards, are you?" Stretton garbled into his coddled eggs. "More at home with a pistol in your hand than a delicate cue."

Asher readied to refute that statement, but unfortunately the bastard spoke the truth.

Turnip blathered on… "Much the same, I expect, with all the gentlemanly pursuits – boxing, riding to hounds, swordsmanship. I mean, prattling with bayonet or pistol is hardly the same as the genteel art of fencing, is it?"

Asher felt his own lips curve in tandem with Lucas's.

"I believe, ladies, gentlemen, wife," Lucas said with a satisfied smile, "that I have chosen tonight's entertainment."

I COULDN'T HAVE THOUGHT OF A BETTER IDEA MYSELF

"Do you know what Lucas has planned for this evening?" asked Lily as she walked arm in arm with Rosalind down the hallway towards the Great Portrait Gallery. "He was sitting upon thorns about it last night."

"I have some idea, considering missing items, an excited Robert, noisy dragging of furniture and the early tea Lucas insisted we all have."

Lily nodded, still bewildered.

When the ladies had returned from the village, a mysterious message had been pinned up on the pistachio-green wall of the drawing room, detailing that the gentlemen would be unavailable for the afternoon, that only a light tea would be served at around five and that the ladies' presence would be required in the Gallery precisely on the hour of six. Skittles perhaps? Shuttlecock?

Following behind, the other ladies chatted excitedly. Stretton's sister, who really was the dearest of girls, laughed with a few neighbours who were also staying on as house guests, while Lucas's mother and another widow from London compared jewellery.

Two footmen stood in front of the Portrait Gallery doors and as the ladies approached, they swept a low bow, bidding them enter.

Usually crammed with tables, chairs and other bits and bobs of furniture without a home, the long narrow hall had been cleared, except for the chaises, which had been pushed to the very edges. Candelabras blazed with light, set upon tables in front of the windows, and every single wall sconce had been lit.

Faces, some smiling, some sad, gazed down from the portraits, all eyes smug at their knowledge of the evening's entertainment.

"Gracious alive," Lily uttered, before a footman escorted them to a comfortable chaise with plumped cushions. A table to the side held chilled bottles, glasses, bowls of sugar plums, confectionery and biscuits.

"I know why I married Lucas when I see such wonderful organisation," Rosalind said as she chewed on a pink bonbon, handing Lily a flute of champagne.

A round of applause diverted her attention as Lucas entered the room.

Lily rather gawped at seeing her host and friend in such a state of…undress. No cravat or jacket adorned his person, not even a waistcoat. And his feet were entirely bare! A billowing white shirt and breeches were all he wore – practically naked. In fact, she was sure she'd never seen Mr Mereworth in less.

He did, however, look mightily impressive, his powerful build seemingly more suited to less clothing, with browned muscular throat bared for the ladies' delectation, thighs straining at the tight attire.

"Hmm," murmured Rosalind appreciably, "and that's the other reason I married him."

Swatting her hand, Lily reclined on the luxurious silk chaise to listen.

"Please forgive my indecent attire," Lucas said, sketching a hand down his shirt, "and that of my fellow competitors', but for your entertainment tonight, we shall endeavour to show our skills at fencing."

"Oh, still my beating heart," said Rosalind, fanning a hand over her face.

Lily gulped and concurred, but then wondered if that had been sarcasm.

Yet who was she most eager to view in only shirt and breeches?

The answer should be obvious: Jack with his sable looks, her potential candidate for number eight, but all that kept flashing before her eyes was Asher and that tall, taut body.

But how were Asher's swordsmanship skills? He'd admitted he only enjoyed games of intelligence, so mayhap this was not his forte, and clearly, not all the gentlemen were fencing as some had lined up against the window, including little Robert who looked fit to burst with excitement.

Asher was not amongst them.

"A series of ten bouts will be displayed for your enjoyment," Lucas continued, "and ladies, you must decide the two most skilled. For added spice, those two gentlemen will remove the blossom from their tips and battle with sharp foils for the last match."

Tension was palpable as all the men entered from another door – it was like a gladiator match of old. Lily tried not to stare at all the half-naked participants and instead scrutinised the floor, but she'd never seen so many nude feet either. The unmarried Catherine Stretton was also transfixed, eyeing Sir John with an avid gleam, and indeed all the gentlemen looked very fine.

Rosalind reached behind and grabbed a red, woollen blanket to cover their laps – the men really had thought of everything.

This evening's first engagement involved Lucas, and not a sound could be heard as he and a neighbour faced each other *en guard*. The contenders wore leather vests, despite their blunted foils, but a sense of danger still surrounded them in the wood-panelled gallery, bloodthirsty ancestors gazing down. There seemed something so primal about it all.

Without further ado, metal clashed upon metal as the two men lunged, parried, their swords sliding and skimming. They danced along the narrow hallway, foils shimmering so fast it was hard to follow the movement.

Lucas was a tall, brawny fellow, but in this sport, he emerged as grace personified – agile and light. His stance appeared so natural, as though he had been born with a sword in his hand, and finally a bungled lunge from the neighbour brought an end to the battle as Lucas pricked his shoulder.

The two gentlemen bowed to the ladies and as a flushed Rosalind clapped enthusiastically, she twisted to Lily. "Lucas and I might skip supper tonight. Do you think you might be able to supervise?"

"I WAS TAUGHT PERSONALLY by Angelo the Younger," jabbered Stretton as Asher leaned against a portrait of a bored pug. "In fact, Angelo said he'd never seen such an upright stance as mine."

Asher had no doubt that Stretton would be good, although an upright stance could also be considered an insult, but the turnip's constant bluster felt incredibly wearing. Still, good preparation for the House of Lords.

Instead, he concentrated on analysing Sir John and Winterbourne. The young baronet fenced adeptly, but the marquess's battle strategy consisted of speed and energy – skill was useless if your opponent gave you no time to apply it.

"Angelo stated it's the noble *blue* blood within me," Turnip continued. "Of course, the aristocratic lines keep getting diluted by all these" – a disdainful gaze raked Asher – "toadying cits."

Yawning, Asher eyed the man. He'd love to tell him that he wasn't only a common cit but a former valet too...

"You're next, Lord Rainham. Give 'im a drubbin'," little Robert piped up, and he peeled himself from the wall to greet the triumphant marquess.

"Ah hah," Winterbourne bellowed. "My youth versus your experience."

Meanwhile, the ladies, after an initial period of trepidation and awe, were now behaving worse than the young bucks at Angelo's fencing academy and indulging in raucous catcalls. Rosalind seemed to be taking bets and Miss Catherine Stretton had clapped at every thrust or parry.

Earlier, his own match against a neighbour of Lucas's had gone well, although the man had only been mediocre proficient. Asher hadn't even broken a sweat.

Concentration, however, had nearly cracked at feeling Lily's eyes upon him.

Did she like what she saw? Certainly, he was toned and fit, but the Marquess of Winterbourne was over ten years younger than he, and her gaze had equally perused his agile posturing...he'd happened to notice.

Buckling on the leather vest, Asher debated tactics. Winterbourne fought swiftly but tended to leave himself open, and he also never let up, never stepped back for a moment, to think, to conserve energy.

Sir John handed him the weapon. "Good luck, Lord Rainham. He's so fast. I could hardly get a strike in."

Swishing his foil, Asher stood back, relishing again the feel of it in his hand, the hilt commissioned specially for his long fingers.

Short sword, sabre, colichemarde – he was adept with each, and always travelled with a selection. After all, in his profession, one could never be too careful, but this particular weapon was a favourite, and he loved the skill of fencing, the intelligence, the stratagem.

Winterbourne cricked an eyebrow as they stood *en guard*, but it wasn't long before Asher had to parry, as the man came forward like the devil possessed, his sprightly feet dancing upon the wooden floor, foil held perfectly loose in his grip.

Having withstood the initial onslaught, Asher pressed on the attack, forcing a retreat but the marquess always managed to keep his balance and poise...and then assail again.

Adjusting his stance to combat the constant barrage, Asher lunged at an opening but in a flash, Jack deflected, their bodies and swords meeting and sliding.

It was then that Asher knew.

Winterbourne was tiring. Sweat plastered his hair,

breathing laboured and black eyes slightly wild. Soon, he would make a mistake.

They both fell back. "Come along, young Winterbourne," chided Asher. "Keep your sword up."

"Never had any complaints before," the rogue snorted, and battle commenced once more.

"I THINK we should have a scoring system," suggested Rosalind, as they watched the two men duet along the floor.

"Hmm? With points for fencing moves and such," Lily replied distractedly. She couldn't take her eyes off either man. They were both so graceful. Winterbourne struck with a ferocity that belied his affable nature, and yet Asher punished the slightest weakness with strange, controlled flicky strokes that defied the eye. "But I don't know what any of the moves are called."

From the corner of her eye, she noticed the betting notebook come out again.

"Neither do I. No, I was thinking more…" Rosalind chewed the end of her pencil. "We will assign up to ten points in each category. Headings such as… Muscle." She wrote down, underlining it several times. "Agility. Strength. Fervour. Stamina. Control."

Lily wrinkled her brow. "Why?"

"Well, I thought it might assist you in deciding whom to seduce for the accomplishment of resolution number eight. I'm sure all this swordplay is really to show us how proficient they'd be in bed."

"What!" Lily's mouth gaped. "Rosalind, I am not bedding a man simply because he's agile with a sword!"

"But why not? Isn't that the point? Don't you want to complete your list?"

"No, I also want..."

She almost said intelligence and wit and hazel eyes, but there lay the danger – to her heart. "It's a good idea, actually," she instead acknowledged. "Jack does seem to be winning on most counts."

Feeling guilty for no good reason, she fixed her gaze on the men again. Never had she seen so much muscle and sinew flex in places she really shouldn't be viewing. Thighs, buttocks...

Asher suddenly fell into retreat as his opponent battled forward, although to be honest, even in retreat, Asher looked...in control, a fierce concentration marking his brow.

"Hmm," replied Rosalind, scratching her auburn hair with the end of her pencil. "I'll give Jack ten points each for strength and fervour, but we shall see."

Unexpectedly, Asher skidded on the floor, falling to one knee, and Lily's heart ceased beating as Jack descended like an avenging spirit, sword swashing, but Asher abruptly rolled, jumping to nimble feet as gasps echoed around the hall from the ladies.

The combat changed tone, with Jack now defending a never-ending series of valiant strikes and deft swishes, until finally with a pressing lunge and a peculiar turn of Asher's wrist, Jack lost his sword. It looped into the air, only to fall clattering in front of the ladies, who first cried out and then stood to their feet in riotous applause.

"Oh," gasped Rosalind, nudging Lily hard in the side. "That's maximum points to Asher for stamina, control and agility."

THERE ARE NO WINNERS…

"You weren't trying," Asher observed as he helped Lucas unbuckle the vest after his defeat.

All ten battles had now been fought, and although the strength of some combatants had waned, not overtly and never that of Major Lucas Mainwaring.

A wry grin graced his friend's face. "Well, I've already basted Stretton in the aristocratic stakes so I thought you should thrash him in the fencing…if you've impressed the ladies enough. And you know what happened the last time we two fenced in seriousness."

Yes, he did. They'd fought for hours – even Angelo had gone home, and eventually after calling it quits, they'd gone to an alehouse. "Stretton's good though. Better than I expected."

Lucas merely smiled again and strode to the highly appreciative audience. "Well, ladies. Have you decided on the final two?"

Stepping forward, Rosalind kissed her husband's scarred, sweaty cheek. "Firstly, I would like to say thank you to Lucas for a superb evening's entertainment."

Enthusiastic female hurrahs boomed around the gallery, amplified by the amount of champagne consumed. "Your sword has been truly impressive tonight, my lord husband."

"Thank you, my Lady Helmdon. My sword is, as always, at your disposal."

"Hmm, yes, swords aside, the ladies have voted unanimously for the two undefeated competitors. Lord Stretton." The man swaggered forward, foil in limp hand. "And Lord Rainham. Our two viscounts must battle it out."

"Rainham," barked Stretton, "what say we make it a touch more stimulating and do without the leather vests? Or are you afraid of a little prick?"

Rosalind snorted, but Asher's thought processes were already in motion.

A hundred probabilities rushed through his head as he weighed up the risks, mentally cataloguing Stretton's strengths and weaknesses. The man had last fenced, so was tired. Being slightly heavier, he had power but lacked grace. An upright stance gave him poise but he lacked fluidity. He'd insulted Lily at dinner.

The ladies stood, awaiting Asher's response, but he now pondered on a new sensation. Never in his life had he felt peer pressure as he'd always relied on his internal system of probability and therefore had never taken any notice of disappointed faces.

But today an uncharacteristic impulse ran down his spine – to sod the odds and just thrash the annoying bugger.

Why? Why did he feel that way?

He spied Lily, her crystal-blue eyes wide – he liked to think in worry – her chest rising in agitated pants.

Perplexed, he frowned. Was he doing this for a woman? How baffling.

"Agreed," he said. "There is only a three in ten chance of a mortal wound."

Lily wanted to scream. To protest it was senseless male posturing, but Rosalind pulled her back to the chaise.

Three in ten was too high. A thrust to the chest and his lung could be pierced.

"Rosalind, I think you should stop this," she fretted. Christmas was supposed to be a time of goodwill but instead two grown men were about to engage with deadly swords.

"Lily, look at me." A soft hand clasped her chin. "Asher is no foolish unlicked cub. He knows what he's doing."

"I..." She glanced over to the men.

Undeniably, Asher did express an air of...calm. All the laces on his shirt were loose, baring the top of his chest and some slight hair, and she couldn't help the pleasurable ripple that ran through her, despite the fear.

Never had she seen Mr Mereworth's chest. Even when he'd been ill with his mortal fever, he had insisted that only his valet see to his needs, and yet Asher stood tall and proud, using a towel to dry his bare throat. Her mouth dried as she followed the trail of that towel to his linen-clad chest, his slender hips and long, long legs.

He looked so awfully...male. And the sensations he elicited within her were previously unknown. Mr Mereworth had been handsome and she'd felt...want, but he'd always been placed on a self-imposed pedestal and she'd never been allowed to touch.

Asher appeared so very touchable.

"Rosalind... Does gazing at Lucas in this state of dress make you feel all..."

"Squirmy?"

"Yes, that's the word."

"Hmm. Quite so. 'Tis all that unleashed virile power and potent strength. Phew," she said, pressing another bumper glass of champagne into Lily's hand. "Have more of this. It will either help or hinder the squirmy feeling."

Gulping, she watched the two viscounts as they came to the middle of the hall. Stretton smirked whilst Asher stood so casual, laughing with Jack and fiddling with his sleeves.

"En guard," the men said, adopting their positions.

Lily tried to heed her friend's reassurance but worry still churned as swords began to clash.

Their styles seemed so different – Stretton was both aggressive and skilled, foil always stabbing at his opponent and, after all, he had beaten Lucas.

Asher fought gracefully, his wiry body loose and fluid, and even his free hand looped elegantly behind him, those long fingers sweeping and curling as though over a woman's back.

What would it feel like to have that hand caressing at...

Rosalind budged her, and she realised that Lucas and Robert had joined them. Despite his perspiring appearance, Lucas sat next to his wife and tried to persuade Robert to sit on his knee, but the lad gave him a look of utter incredulousness and leaned against the chaise arm instead.

Slashing metal grated their ears as Stretton lunged and Asher blocked. The women gasped. Robert gawked. Lily closed her eyes and quaffed champagne.

"Stop worrying, Lily," a rasping voice whispered. "Asher's playing with him."

"Playing!" she hissed, rather too loudly. "Stretton beat you, Lucas."

"Hmm," murmured Rosalind. "Did he? You were a little cow-handed with that last manoeuvre."

"I did what was best, my rose. But truthfully, Lily, *L'École des Armes* is bedtime reading for Asher. In fact," he confided, "the late Angelo senior told me Asher had such grace as to make the angels weep."

Feeling a touch mollified, Lily took a long breath. The more she now studied them, the more she could see that Asher was biding his time, his eyes constantly scrutinising the other's wrist movements, and he never made uncalculated swipes.

He waited. Watched.

Stretton suddenly thrust with a powerful lunge to the stomach but it was nimbly waved aside, and as the man's hand flew out, Asher made his strike, drawing a streak of red down Stretton's upper arm.

"First blood to Lord Rainham. Swords down, gentlemen," Jack called over the unruly applause.

"Oh look," Asher commented to an angry-faced Stretton, "your blood's red, just like mine."

THE CONGRATULATING CROWD surrounded Asher with hearty thumps to his back and the occasional pinch of his arse, from whom he wasn't quite sure. Possibly Lucas's mother, who was well and truly stewed to the gills.

But he knew it wasn't Lily.

All the combatants shared a drink and he even received a handshake from the defeated Stretton who admitted he'd never seen the like. The flattery felt curious to Asher as it was simply a matter of heeding one's training and following logic.

And following was what he'd do now because after Lily had commiserated with Jack and Stretton, she'd vanished down one of the halls. And for some strange reason, that hurt.

Did she dislike the violence? Did she think him abhorrent?

Wandering the tangle of panelled passageways, he noticed a side alcove held light and so hunted its source, rounding the corner to find Lily gazing at a portrait of a stag. She was muttering to herself. "Damn stags, the lot of them..."

"Lily?"

She twisted, and his body shuddered in response. A lantern was held aloft in one of her hands and in the other a half glass of champagne. Blond locks fell from the elegant coiffure of earlier, slightly dishevelled in a manner he'd never seen before. She looked as though she'd recently been tumbled...or was about to be.

"Are you following me?"

He chanced the odds of being truthful against lying. "Yes," he replied.

"Why?" She gulped champagne, lips glistening with moisture.

Indeed, why had he followed her? Hurt pride? Bloody hell, this was pathetic, but she was turning his wits inside out. "I don't really know, but I worried the fighting had discomfited you. Why were you muttering about stags?"

"I was thinking you men are like them – strutting around to show who has the biggest...antlers or sword, is there a difference?"

Asher strutted nearer and took the champagne glass

from her hand, bringing it to his mouth and tasting. In this low light, her eyes shimmered as she watched his throat swallow.

"Am I the dominant stag then?" he enquired. "Would you be my chosen doe?"

"You should find someone younger," she retorted, tugging a stray curl.

Something inordinately primal ran through Asher's body, just as he'd thought himself immune to such feelings. Certainly, he'd felt lust in the past, but never this all-consuming desire to hold, taste, take.

"I think the victorious stag gets to select whoever he desires. Were you worried for me, Lily?" he abruptly asked, remembering her agitated look of before.

"Of course I was worried, you ignoramus," she snapped. "Three in ten chance of death, you said. That's below your limit!"

Extremely pleased with her anger, Asher reached out a hand and snatched a hairpin that stuck from her curls. Oddly, he hadn't processed the chances that a single pin would undermine the entire foundations of her coiffure, and he watched awestruck as the tumble of locks cascaded around her shoulders and down her back – a river of soft wheat.

"Oh Lily. Your hair is glorious."

"Is it?" She frowned. "Mr Mereworth said it belonged on a harlot and I always had to plait it at night."

Asher stared, unsure how to react. Had her husband been a cork-brained nodcock?

"Does that mean you've never felt a man's fingers brush through those curls?"

She shook her head, and Asher acted on instinct for once.

Taking the lantern from her and placing it on the table with her glass, he then stroked a palm down those glossy locks.

It slipped as though on silk, and he brought his other hand up to more firmly drag through the pale strands, watching the play of curls over his darker skin.

A soft inhalation answered his action and without even thinking on the odds of rejection, he slowly lowered his mouth. With scarcely an inch between their lips, he hesitated, waiting for a sign that he wasn't alone in this indefinable feeling.

Her breath hitched, blue eyes searing enough to induce frostbite, but still he waited.

Rose-pink lips parted, and then he waited no longer because she narrowed the breach, met his mouth, and he kissed Lily Mereworth.

Flavoured with champagne and almonds, her succulent lips felt soft and sweet, and he twisted a hand in her fallen curls, tipping her head to better angle his kiss.

All evening he'd sweated with sword, but his lust didn't give a damn for his state and neither did Lily, it seemed, as she reached out a hand to touch his throat, her fingers casually wandering down the open neck of his shirt.

His body hardened and his arms responded, hauling her against his chest, one hand entangled at her delicate nape, the other at her waist. Lily's suppleness felt utterly magnificent and he plundered her mouth, deepening the kiss until neither could breathe.

"Lily…" he groaned as she pressed against him, her fingers raking at his shoulders. Asher tried to summon one good reason as to why he shouldn't lift her up and find a room, any room, but could think of none.

Unbidden, his hand grabbed at her satin skirts, but

sudden muffled laughter filtered through the labyrinth of corridors, followed by a female shriek.

They both stilled in the shadowed alcove, as motionless as hunted deer, and looked towards the sound.

Illuminated by a scattering of wall sconces at the far end of the panelled corridor, a flash of aquamarine met the wall, before it was pounced upon by Lucas.

Unlike themselves, no preamble was necessary between husband and wife, and they tore at each other, fists clasping hair, mouths melded, bodies grinding.

Noting Rosalind's foot slide up Lucas's leg and then Lucas's hand slide down Rosalind's derrière, Asher could only see it concluding one way, and he drew back from Lily, letting her radiant hair spill from his grip.

Confusion crumpled his brow at the look of utter wretchedness on her face as she turned from the fervent couple and glanced up at him.

"Lily?" he murmured. But she violently pulled away, fist to her mouth.

"Leave me alone," she whispered, tears glistening in her eyes, lip quivering. "Leave me alone, Lord Rainham."

And she twisted to run from his wanting body and turbulent mind.

ARE YOU UNDER THERE, ASHER?

"Foolish, foolish woman," Lily berated her pale features in the hand mirror. "Will you never learn."

Black circles loitered beneath her eyes, despite it now being nigh on afternoon. Dreams had tormented her last night. Asher in every single one, and she swore his citrus cologne still lingered in her hair.

She sank back on the bed after throwing more logs on the fire, mind so overset she'd forgotten to use the embroidered screen to protect her pale complexion. Although what was the use anyway? There would be no one to see her reddened nose today as she'd retired to her room in wretchedness and confusion.

Dearest Rosalind had come to visit earlier, bringing mint tea for her supposed sick stomach, and she'd eyed Lily suspiciously but not commented on her woebegone expression and puffy face.

A dalliance – that was all number eight was ever meant to be. Some light-hearted affair she could laugh about sophisticatedly with said lover long after the event. It was a number to be ticked, a date to be added, a vindication that she had changed her life, become who she always wanted to be – spirited and alive, that no man would ever again smother her voice, her will, her desires.

She liked her new-found independence: investing, studying business journals, and reading frivolous novels until midnight with no one to complain about the expensive usage of candles.

And Asher threatened all that.

Maybe she was being arrogant. Maybe Asher only wished for a brief affair too, but her instincts screamed otherwise. He was not some young whippersnapper that played with women, nor a rakish rogue searching for an evening's entertainment.

She sensed Asher would expect all of a woman if he were to take a mistress – he was not a man for half-measures.

Watching him battle Stretton last night, she had seen a confident, highly intelligent, intense man. It both thrilled and frightened the life out of her.

And as for last night's kiss… Oh, she had never felt the like.

The overwhelming craving, the firmness of his mouth, those long fingers dragging over her hair, his aroused body pressing so close. She could lose herself in such desire. Lose all sense of judgement. He need only snap his fingers and she would fall to his feet for such a kiss, waiting pitifully for more.

She had waited in such a way for Mr Mereworth.

Not for passion, but for kindness, regard, small signs of affection. At the beginning, he had said he'd loved her, but that she'd needed some…polish, some refinement, as he had put it.

And she had tried. Always, she had tried so very hard to be the woman he'd wanted: the perfect hostess, the adept housekeeper, the quiet wife, the proper lady. But never had it been enough.

She had laughed too loudly, folded the linens incorrectly, not reprimanded the kitchen boy strongly enough, spoke foolishness... The list had been endless. And so, she'd tried harder and harder until she'd become... nothing. Merely quoting to all and sundry Mr Mereworth's underlined advice in *Miss Pikesworth's guide to Etiquette.*

If she became entangled with Asher, he might ask her to cease investing – men didn't seem to like women earning their own money. He might casually suggest she stop reading scandalous novels and give her more edifying material. She might even agree – if only to feel that kiss, that passion.

She would lose herself yet again.

Lily pulled the coverlet over her head and considered staying there until Christmas was over. According to Rosalind, most people had arisen late after the tardiness of last night, and the day was being spent on gentle pursuits: reading, catching up with letters and walking the estate if one felt thus energised.

Tomorrow would be busy enough with St Thomas's Day, as the kitchens were being set up to receive anyone that wished food, and sacks of flour and dried goods stood ready. The men were to distribute alms in the surrounding villages to the infirm or elderly whilst the ladies would assist here at Helmdon Court.

In fact, she thought, with slightly more cheer, it should be entirely possible to avoid Lord Rainham for all of today and tomorrow, as Sir John's inventive choice of entertainment tonight was to take the men to the village inn. For the women, under the command of Catherine Stretton…hat trimming.

Over turquoise beribboned bonnets, she would banish every thought of Asher Rainham and focus her attention on her choice of entertainment for Thursday, which would complete another item on her list.

A light knock on the door sounded, and she bade them enter from beneath the coverlet.

The bed dipped.

"Are you coming out of there, Lily?"

"No."

"The men have already left for the inn. Rather early but there you are."

Lily didn't move. She would not be falling for Rosalind's clankers. "I still feel sick," she groused.

"Hmm."

A soft hand patted her through the blanket and with sudden embarrassment, Lily recalled the scene of Rosalind and Lucas devouring each other last night.

But it hadn't solely been their passion that had disconcerted her – it had been their devotion, the utter trust they had in each other. She'd been envious, and there stood in front of her had been Lord Rainham, gazing down with such…

"Lily, did something happen with Asher last night?"

"Why would you ask that?"

"He was a bear with a sore head this morning. Told Lucas that soft eggs had a one in forty chance of killing him, and that there was a nine in ten chance of being discovered tupping one's wife in a hallway when one had guests."

A response was impossible.

"Lily?" The voice questioned softly. "Did you complete number eight by any chance?"

"No!" She shot out from under the blankets to find Rosalind sniggering. Lily scowled. "That was unfair."

"So why are you being all…like the old Mrs Mereworth? Sick stomach and hiding. Next you'll be quoting George."

"How are the preparations for St Thomas's Day proceeding? Can I assist in any way?"

"Lily…"

She sighed. "I… I like him. I like Asher. Are you happy? And therefore, he has to be excluded from my list of candidates for achieving this most problematic number eight."

Rosalind crossed her eyes, making Lily chuckle.

"That is the oddest thing I've ever heard. You *are* supposed to like the man you seduce."

"Yes, like them, not…"

"Hmm?"

"He's so…"

"Hmm?"

"Singular. Unique. I wanted a normal, average libertine to assist me with number eight."

Snorting, Rosalind patted her hand. "You don't want normal and average in bed, Lily. You want impassioned, vehement" – she flung her arms out – "adoring, zealous and…huge."

Lily dissolved into giggles – what else could she do? Rosalind was such a shocking influence and yet had such cheer despite her pained and difficult childhood.

"That's better, Lily. I would so hate to see the old Mrs Mereworth return. The new you is fun, bold and does not hide under the coverlet, unless…" Rosalind gasped, a stunned expression forming. "Or is Asher under there with you? Am I being played for a fool?" She patted the sheets frantically. "Are you under there, Asher? Are you putting that agile body to good use?"

"Stop, I can't…" Lily spluttered, wiping her eyes. "Oh, thank you, Rosalind, for chasing away my blue devils. It can be so hard to unhitch the past, but you are right, I have been dwelling and fretting for no reason."

"Exactly. Now come and play with little Alice. She's chewing chair legs today. Then we'll discuss the Christmas food and think about presents for the children."

Rosalind stood and made for the door. "By the way," she called, as she reached for the handle, "the new Lily said last year that she would embrace all new adventures." Glancing back, she winked. "And that does not preclude adventures of the heart."

The door closed, and Lily collapsed back onto the bed.

Thoughts of Asher returned but this time she didn't banish them. She reminisced on his expression of want as he'd bent down to kiss her, the gaze of awe as her hair had tumbled down, his groan of desire when she'd surged against him.

All adventures?

TO WOO OR NOT TO WOO...

"How does one go about wooing a lady?"

The look of utter disbelief Asher received for his question was demeaning. Did everyone consider him dead from the waist down. He wasn't that emotionless, was he?

"Erm." Lucas seemed to put some thought into it as he drained the dregs of his ale and shifted uneasily on the bench. "Dunno. A murder hunt worked for me, but probably not advisable for all."

Asher let his head drop to the table. No, he couldn't kill anyone, that would cause further problems, although Stretton was a potential candidate. The fellow had bounced back from his trouncing with *joie de vivre* and could currently be heard patronising the locals at the bar with how his predecessor had saved the king, rescued the country, defeated all evils, twaddle, bosh, piffle...

"Never mind," Asher said with a sigh.

"Who are you wooing?" Lucas's words stumbled. "Damn, that's difficult to say after four pints."

"No one. I don't think she's interested. I'm probably too old."

"Too… Asher, you have the strength and stomach muscles of men half your age. Don't be such a pudding."

"Pudding?" Sir John abruptly raised his head from its resting place in the crook of his arm. "Is it Christmas?"

"Inn, John. Remember? All your inspired idea."

"Oh, yes. I'd thought to try and bond with Stretton over a pint, but he doesn't think me, a mere baronet, good enough for his sister."

"Hell's teeth," grouched Lucas. "All this women trouble. You two need the advice of someone with more experience than me. And where the hell's my next ale?"

Coquettish laughter drifted to their ears and they all turned to view the comely barmaid blush as Winterbourne leaned – or was that leered – over the wooden counter. He waggled his fingers, beckoning her close, and she did as he bade, poor deluded innocent, giggling as the rogue whispered in her ear.

"Oy!" shouted Lucas. "Stop wooing the maids and fetch the ales, damn it. Priorities, man, priorities."

Asher smiled, arranging the empty tankards to the edge of the table. "Double tongue, my friend. Your priorities were much the same last night. Must be the cold weather."

"At least she's my wife…and 'tis my house. And besides, you shouldn't have been lurking in a dark alcove either. I presume it was the fair Lily in your clutches?"

"Hmm," Asher replied non-committedly.

"I should warn you," Lucas continued with a benign expression, "that if you break Lily's heart, I will have to cut your gizzards out. After Rosalind has been at you, of course."

"I wouldn't worry. I don't think I have that ability."

"What, to break hearts? Of course you do. Everyone does. Rosalind carved mine out with a blunt spoon."

"You're nauseatingly content now though."

"It took time, patience and use of my noggin. Women's ways are mysterious."

Asher swigged his ale. "It's so abnormal for me… But I want to see Lily smile, make her laugh, touch her…"

Lucas looked bemused. "Never thought I'd see the day."

Frowning, Asher analysed the sensations within. Despite what his men thought, he'd enjoyed lovers before, but it had always been a matter of itches to be scratched, not this…

"She makes me feel peculiar."

"Who's peculiar?" asked Jack, finally returning with the ale. "I like peculiar. Life can be dull enough."

"Dull? The life of a rake?" enquired Lucas. "Your exploits with that Russian widow travelled all the way here to the Northamptonshire gossip columns."

"Don't believe everything you read in those rags… That was only the half of it." Jack grinned, clasping his chest. "But alas, my heart is fickle."

Lucas made room on the bench. "Well, my lascivious friend, there are two men here that need the advice of an experienced rogue."

"Ah, I'm good at this."

Asher winced.

The rogue sat. "Using my powers of deduction, I will surmise it is the pretty Catherine and the delectable Lily that are causing all the problems, yes?"

Both men vaguely bobbed their heads.

"Well," he said with gusto, "the entertainment I have decided upon for tomorrow night will allow you both to enact rule thirteen – the displaying of one's protective instincts. Last night, the ladies saw your manly side – rule six, by the way – but tomorrow you will both have the opportunity to demonstrate your inner softness. Women love that."

"Rules?" Lucas chuckled. "Inner bloody softness? What a load of balderdash."

Jack merely smirked. "I never receive the thanks I deserve. Now then, Rainham, you need to find out about this mysterious list of Lily's."

Lucas's ale spluttered over the table.

"List?" Asher frowned.

"Hmm. I have heard whisperings that Mrs Lily Mereworth has a list of resolutions with a curious uncompleted number eight."

"A list? Eight? How did you find out?" Asher cursed his stupid question. He'd trained the man himself. "Don't answer that. And, Lucas, you obviously know something too?"

"Rosalind would kill me. Or even worse, withhold certain privileges. I know nothing. I've heard nothing. I've seen nothing."

"The original monkey," Asher remarked. "Well, I can be sure you'll never reveal information under torture, so, a drinking contest it is."

"And what if I win?" asked Lucas, sullenly.

"I'll guarantee the non-disclosure of your code name to your wife."

"Done."

THE BEAR and Ragged Staff Inn shook with merriment as Asher attempted to throw a small disc at some pins. He missed.

"Senseless game," he muttered to himself as he downed another quart of beer.

As hoarfrost had painted the small windows white, so the inn had filled with a crowd of villagers braving the cold and dark for some warmth – inside and out. The sight of bosky nobles playing the frankly incomprehensible local game of hooded skittles must have merely topped off their evening.

Asher leaned himself against the flaking limewash of the stone wall and hoped the horses knew the path back to Helmdon Court as none of them would find a Frenchman in Paris with all the liquor they'd quaffed.

Watching Lucas destroy another set of pins, Asher breathed deeply, enjoying the bittersweet aroma of ale and wood smoke that swirled about him.

It had been decided by Sir John that the drinking contest should involve various games and these skittles were the third.

Earlier, Asher had figured out a not-very-puzzling puzzle cup. The aim had been to glug all the liquor contained within, without spilling any from the various spouts that riddled it. Drinking last had helped, as he'd been able to scrutinise the exits whilst the other fellows got soaked.

As fate would have it, winning that game had ruined his chances at the next, the belly of wine having taken its toll.

Sir John had won the second, a seemingly pointless exercise involving a bull's horn attached to the wall and a piece of rope – and people dared to call *him* peculiar.

Now they were amusing themselves with a version of miniature skittles. It was familiar to him but played on the strangest of tables, having cushioned walls to the left, right and rear, and also sporting a curved hood of leather which stretched over the top. These developments thus presented further options...

Lucas threw the disc to resounding cheers. It bounced off the roof, hit the two sides, before flattening the remaining skittles.

The bugger.

It would appear there would be no revealing of Lily's mysterious list from Lucas, so he wandered instead to the blazing fire and stared into the flames, warming his hands.

Never did he expect, at the age of three and forty, to meet a woman who so fascinated him. Desire, regard and esteem all blended into the strangest need.

In past times, he'd felt those individual emotions for females but never all at once.

And what did this fascination mean? A liaison? He didn't think so as not only did he want to bed Lily Mereworth, but also to get trounced at cards, watch her read, hear about her investments. Mayhap, they could become long-term lovers, but somehow that lacked devotion.

But devotion would mean...

"You won't find any answers in there," Jack consoled.

Asher lifted his eyes from the flames. "I don't believe Lucas will be forfeiting any information this evening."

"Don't worry. I'll ask around the servants. Rule twenty-three – thoroughly research one's quarry. And if not, my chosen entertainment will set you up nicely."

"Dare I ask?"

Jack grinned, his usual debonair self still looking debonair even with loosened cravat and ale on his shirt. "The ladies are fiddle-faddling with bonnets tonight, so I'd imagine they'll be all agog for our company tomorrow.

That Lady Sidlow's a saucy piece, and I'm hoping she'll have room in her Christmas garters for me."

"Lord Winterbourne, you are a rogue."

"I know," he said with a waggish wink, "but the very best sort."

LUCAS ATTEMPTED to enter the master bedchamber with the silence of a mouse; after all, he'd once reconnoitred an entire mansion in Paris without waking the occupants.

Bootless, he tiptoed across the plush rug. A chair, which had appeared in the middle of the room, proved awkward and stubbing his toe on the bed leg caused some anguish, but he finally made it, following the scent of roses and…greenery.

He might have been able to forestall the Christmas decorations in the rest of the house, but their chamber was a different matter. The lush freshness assailed his senses and rested his mind.

After peeling back the coverlet, he sank down onto the soft mattress, almost groaning in pleasure.

"Lucas?"

"Back to the land of nod, my sweet," he murmured, but a hand wandered to his chest.

"Did you have a nice evening?"

"Hmm. I missed you."

"Liar." Rosalind laughed, slumberous and low. "Did Asher mention Lily?"

"Er…"

"Yes, then. That's good."

"How are the children?"

"Alice tried to eat a pine cone and Robert told me to bugger off."

Pulling her slender body tight, he soothed her shoulder. What were they to do for Robert? A lad so withdrawn and incensed with life. He wouldn't wear the clothes they'd given him, he'd thrown a book at the tutor they'd hired... and he'd told Rosalind to bugger off.

When he forgot to act in such a way, he was a superb lad, bright and brave. Surely with time he would come to trust them. They just had to keep trying until he lowered his fierce guard.

Sighing, Lucas closed his eyes.

BIRDS AND THE BEES...

'I twist my legs round his naked loins, the flesh of which, so firm, so...'

Goodness.

Lily placed the book face down on the dressing table and fanned her heated cheeks as the maid fiddled with the complicated chignon.

The bold lady involved in that amorous scene would have accomplished number eight without so much as a "How do you do?"

Fluffing her sleeve, Lily exiled the wicked book to the further reaches of her mind. Dinner was being served slightly later tonight, after which they would enjoy Jack's unknown evening entertainment.

"Would you like more curls loose?" the girl asked. "'Tis a shame to tie them back so fiercely."

About to decline, Lily recalled Asher's reaction to her blond mop and surveyed herself in the mirror. She'd always followed the latest fashion as Mr Mereworth had insisted – torturing her hair into corkscrew ringlets and often painful complicated styles.

The maid smiled at her hesitation and took a section down, smoothing it over her shoulder. Then she took more strands from the front, unpinning and letting them settle around her face. It rendered her younger, more carefree.

"You don't think it makes me look…" Trollopy was what she wished to ask, but although Matilda was an absolute dear, such intimacy was maybe not appropriate.

"'Tis very pretty." Matilda smiled, encouragingly. "If I had hair like yours, I'd wear it loose as much as propriety would allow."

Lily glanced up. "And I wish I'd sleek black locks like your own, so likely it is our fate to never be happy with what God gave us."

"True, although I used to hate my brown eyes until my Arthur told me they reminded him of autumn leaves, so I expect it all depends on the family and friends that surround us."

Lily nodded. The maid was as perceptive as the mistress of the house. Being encompassed by love and kindness shaped and sustained one's self-assurance, but the negativity of others cast its shadow deep over one's soul.

Her very nearness hubble-bubbled Asher's brain as he tried to think of something worth saying to Lily, seated on his left at the dining table.

If truth be told, he'd be interested to know more about her investments but was aware that wouldn't be very…flirtatious.

He couldn't talk about his own job, and most likely a lady wouldn't appreciate knowing the statistical chance of food poisoning at a Christmas gathering – quite low actually as the cold weather aided meat preservation.

Perhaps he could subtly investigate this matter of a list, as although he hadn't worked in the field for a while, he was still a spymaster for blazes' sake. He opened his mouth.

"Do you always rearrange your cutlery?"

Meeting Lily's ice-blue eyes, he shivered with desire, but how to answer her question, especially as he hadn't been aware of doing it.

Glancing down, he beheld the spoons arranged to width size whilst the knives were sorted sharpest first. Sighing at the forks, which were ordered by prong length, he replied, "It seems I do like things to be in order."

A frown crossed her face and he sensed it had been the wrong thing to say.

"Do you wish people to be in order as well? Do you put them into categories and expect them to adhere to rules?"

Breath caught in his throat at her pointed and, it had to be said, rather harsh question. Piercing, hurt eyes awaited his answer but all of a sudden, Mrs Lily Mereworth fell into place, like a jigsaw when only a few pieces remained – no need to look at the picture, just the shapes and where they fitted.

Someone had slotted Lily into a box – a wrong-shaped box with tight walls and a low ceiling. Probably that husband who'd made her plait her luscious hair at night – stupid bugger.

"Not at all," he refuted, shaking his head. He must explain himself, no waffle. "'Tis true I like material things to be in order, but people cannot be categorised. Each individual has their own skills and dichotomies that should be admired as such. Encouraged, in fact. Many a square man has rounded edges and vice versa, if you see what I mean."

She still looked sceptical, and he didn't blame her…and what happened to no waffle?

Asher sought an example. "Take Jack," he said, pointing to the fellow flirting with Lady Sidlow. "An affable rake? Or a compassionate man? Do you see a humorous libertine or someone who has an almost driven need to help others feel cheerful about life? A contented man? Or a sorrowful one?" He twisted. "And the honourable Miss Catherine Stretton. A quiet reticent mouse? Or will that mouse one day roar? I'd say the latter."

Lily bit her lip. "And you, Lord Rainham. What are your dichotomies?"

"I am tidy in mind yet my writing is disordered. I am both servant and lord. Usually, I understand people very well and yet at times conversation flows over my head, incomprehensible. I enjoy luxury and yet have no curtains at home."

She smiled at the latter. "A wife might fix th– Oh. Not that I meant, I mean…"

"I wouldn't expect my wife to faff with curtains if she hated doing so."

"You wouldn't? Isn't that a woman's work? To make sure it is neat and tidy for when you return. To cater for your needs?"

"The best lockpick I ever knew was a woman. Agile, silent and never caught. She could steal a diamond from under your nose and definitely did not feel a need to cater to anyone."

"What happened to her?" Lily asked, hushed.

"She works for my department now." He paused to move a nudged fork back into line. "So you see, Lily, if I were to marry, my wife would never be categorised. She would be cherished for her own skills, be they lock picking, flower arranging, shooting or…investing."

The scrunched serviette dropped to the table and he watched those pretty blond lashes widen. He hadn't meant to play his hand so early, hadn't meant to reveal himself so rashly, but there it was.

Patience – the virtue he told his men to keep foremost in their minds during all pursuits.

But patience be damned for once.

PICKING up her serviette and folding the edges neatly, Lily felt a little faint.

Did he mean… What did he mean? Did he want…? Surely not. It was too soon to…

His terribly handsome eyes caressed her face, and then he twisted to search for a meat knife in the chaos of cutlery.

Did he want *her* as a wife? Or had she got the wrong end of the staff?

And if she hadn't, then why did he want her? Asher was a viscount and she merely a widow in her mid-thirties. A widow who didn't want to be married again, to ever be obligated again. Marriage would mean loss of freedom, her financial independence…

But her eyes were drawn to the laughter opposite, Rosalind giggling whilst Lucas poked her ribs and made a joke about redheads having a temper.

What would it be like to have that closeness? Someone to share things with, to talk to, to laugh with…to love. Not Mr Mereworth's type of critical love but the one being enacted at this very dinner table.

Rosalind looked up, catching her eye. "Thank you, Lily, for all your help in the kitchens. Did you enjoy St Thomas's Day?"

Shaking off her thoughts, Lily applied herself to the answer. "I did. The war has taken its toll, has it not? And wheat prices are at a premium."

Solemnly, Rosalind nodded. "Mrs Taggart was widowed this year – her husband died at Toulouse – and she has five children under the age of ten."

Indeed, the day had been a humbling lesson.

The less fortunate traditionally went door to door this day, asking for alms, but Rosalind had gone one better and opened up the Helmdon Court kitchens for meals, making sure everyone went home full, merry and with at least a sack of grain.

"Have you seen the amount of holly they've brought in return for the meals?" Rosalind gushed. "Unfortunately, some malcontent of a husband says we have to wait till Christmas Eve to put it all up." She scrunched her nose. "At least we are hunting the woods for greenery tomorrow, so that should satisfy my Christmas longing."

"Rosalind would be trimming the halls in September if she could," Lucas added with a grin.

"Well, we never celebrated Christmas when I was young, and I love it. Such a joyous time of year."

Her husband brushed a gentle kiss upon her cheek at the reminder of Rosalind's past, before whispering in her ear with a look of utter tenderness.

Lily stabbed her beef.

"Speaking of joyous things," Rosalind continued, "have you finished the book I lent you, Lily?"

Do not blush. Do not blush. Do not blush. Get revenge later, Lily repeated in her head.

"No, not yet, *dearest.*"

"What are you reading?" asked Asher.

"It's a nature book, isn't it, Lily?" Rosalind replied instead, lips twitching with suppressed mirth.

Flush rising, Lily closed her eyes. Yes, she supposed the exploits of the courtesan Fanny Hill could in some ways be termed a nature book.

"Hmm," she replied obliquely.

"Does it concern the interaction of species?"

Lily's eyes snapped open to gaze suspiciously at Asher, but his expression appeared honest, and so she replied as such. "There does seem to be rather a lot of interaction, yes."

GHOSTS BOTH PAST AND PRESENT...

"Gather around, everybody."

Lily sat where she was told, a comfortable chaise in the corner that was far enough from the roaring fire for her complexion but near enough to feel its warmth.

After dinner, Lord Winterbourne had led them all to the drawing room where comfortable seating was set in a semi-circle around the hearth. It all looked most cosy and she wondered if they were to tell jokes or roast chestnuts.

On another sofa sat Catherine and Sir John, and she speculated as to how Jack had managed to sit them together without Stretton causing a fuss.

Her speculation lasted until she heard the purring voice of Lady Sidlow. "Oh, Lord Stretton, that's so fascinating," the lady gushed with apparent honesty. "Tell me more of your family's heroic deeds?"

Clever Jack, thought Lily.

He continued directing people. "Our hosts to the left and Asher – you are seated next to Lily."

Sinful Jack. Matchmaking, devilish, sinful Jack.

The chaise felt too small. Asher's body, although slender, was all muscle. She could tell by the way his breeches clung to his thighs when he sat, the material stretching and bulging.

Not that she was looking – her eyes merely happened to be at that level.

"If Henry could snuff the candles except for the one at the very back..."

Lily watched as the footman obeyed, the room growing darker by the moment. A tangible sense of excitement suffused the air, as everyone fell silent and gazed at tonight's provider of entertainment.

A low stool sat before the hearth and Jack rested himself languidly upon it, leaning forward, his features satanic in the glow of the leaping flames. Lily shivered and found her arm brushing Asher's. It really was a very small chaise.

Normally, the curtains would be drawn this late, but they'd been left open, the fast-moving clouds causing flashes of moonlight to flicker the room, and every so often, a sharp gust rattled the shutters.

The mighty Tudor fireplaces had struggled to combat the freezing easterly wind of the day, leaving people wrapped to their chins in shawls and blankets.

"Now," Jack began, "I have many fables with which I could regale you tonight as this county of Northamptonshire is rich in folk law, mystery and a fair few...ghosts."

Lily silently quaked. She wasn't very good with terrifying stories.

From beneath hooded eyes, Jack peered out. "I have been asking all the locals–"

"Well, the barmaids and farmers' wives," interrupted Lucas.

"I will not be revealing my sources," he replied, winking as shadows spilt over the blood-red hearth rug. "But I had to decide betwixt three tales that chill the heart and tremble the soul. Should I tell of the grey lady of Delapré, a shade who haunts that nearby abbey? Or perhaps the legend of Jack of Badsaddle? A stupendously named chap, no relation, who slayed the last wolf in England before meeting his mysterious end in the year of our Lord 1375 or…" Everyone held their breath and his voice deepened to silk. "A different tale. One of a true event that takes place scarcely a few miles from where we now sit… The Hounds of Hell."

Catherine gasped and even in this low light, Lily saw Sir John's hand clutch hers in comfort. She frowned; were these scary tales intended to persuade the ladies into–

"And so it would begin," Jack continued, "on an evening such as this – pitch, murky, comfortless, and with the skeletal hand of ice stretching through the night, the silence rent by the distant barking of hounds in the woods. Wild and ancient. Whilst you may run when you hear their desolate howling, it would be to no avail, for no one can escape once the hunt is on."

A sudden beat of wings rapped the window, and a woman shrieked. Jack smiled, unblinking. "The baying would near, louder and shrill, and in the raven night you may perceive red orbs, steadily gaining speed – nearer and nearer. The moon would only escape for a brief moment from its coat of black and then you'd see…eyes wild with hunger, sharp fangs and hides of matted fur." He paused. The fire flared. "But that is not the sight that would still your heart and stay your feet, for there is more, as behind the wild pack sits their master upon a white horse. Yes, my fearful ones... The headless huntsman."

Lily swallowed a whimper of fright. Lady Sidlow held a hand to her neck. But nobody blinked or stirred. 'Twas as if they'd all been turned to stone.

Clutching her shawl closer, Lily scrunched her eyes shut. She'd forever felt dread of the deep dark, its cavernous sinister shadow. Mr Mereworth had slept in his own adjoining bedchamber, and once she had cried out in fright, but he'd shouted that she was foolish. Foolish and stupid.

Those memories of aloneness returned once more, but she jolted as warmth swamped her clenched fist, and peeping down, she saw Asher's long fingers rub over her cold skin. She watched her own hand unlock, watched his fingers enlace with hers, felt his heat. Not meeting his eyes, she merely accepted his touch and listened.

"Many of you have visited Whittlebury woods, not so far from here and thought it benign and peaceful. Visit at night, however, and you may witness this Infernal Chase. Caught within, it will be your final night spent on this earth, and the last man you ever gaze upon will be the spectral hunt master, calling his hounds to heel...or to feast."

Lily shuddered and felt that hand tighten. Asher shifted yet closer, the entire length of his body grazing her side. His thigh skimmed. His hip pressed. Even his evening shoes lightly brushed.

Impulsively, the moon took its chance to fight the shadows in the room, and a shimmering white glittered through the open curtains. But it gave no comfort, solely enhancing the ethereal glow.

"The Whittlebury legend tells," Jack continued, arms

wide and face dark, "that a young knight fell in love – foolish fellow – with the forest keeper's beautiful daughter. But alas she was a cruel mistress, at first encouraging his ardour, his gifts and his touch, before spurning him. His love continued unabated, but she shredded his poor heart, laughed at his passionate words, displayed other lovers, and generally behaved like a bit of a trollop."

The enraptured audience chuckled, lightening the atmosphere, but Jack gave no respite.

"His pure love turned to naked hate. Craving to disgust. Desire to repulsion. Until finally, he could stand it no more and in desperation and melancholy, he took his own life." Jack shook his bowed head, fists clenched tightly. "Did the beautiful one shed a tear of grief for her dead suitor? No, she laughed at the folly of his love."

With face grave, he sighed. "But such cruelty will never go unpunished, and one night when she trod the path through Whittlebury woods, the sound of ghostly baying cut the dark. The faithless one scurried, twigs snapping beneath her quickening feet, but the snarling grew louder. With pounding heart, she ran faster, faster still, feeling their vile wet breath upon her neck, their fetid heat smothering her nostrils, till she stumbled and fell to the unyielding earth, finally seeing that which pursued her so endlessly – her spectral lover and his demonic pack, his Hounds of Hell falling upon her with ravenous hunger."

At such gruesomeness, Lily's skin prickled, and Asher's fingers trailed up her wrist, lower arm and then slid around her back, curving to her spine and pulling her close.

Gazing across the room, she noticed Rosalind, eyes closed, leaning her head against Lucas's shoulder, his hand tucked tight in her auburn hair.

"And that is not the worst," the storyteller now confided, "for this terrible deed is repeated whenever the moon is bright. She runs again, only to be pursued to her fate. But beware, my friends, for if you should get caught in this hunt, they will show no mercy. Blindness, madness and death will forever be your destiny, carried miles and miles on the backs of those fiendish hounds of Whittlebury woods."

Time stopped. No one moved or sighed or twitched or gasped.

Inwardly, Lily quaked, the ceaselessness of that Infernal Chase haunting her.

Jack peered at their rapt faces, seemingly very satisfied with the fearful expressions.

Slowly, they shook themselves from their stupor, stretching creaking bones and chuckling nervously. Asher's hand didn't move but with returning senses, Lily felt rather anxious and troubled now the story had ended.

A shaky ripple of applause broke out for Jack's wonderful entertainment – what better than a true tale of ghosts before Christmastide.

Still looking mysterious in the fire's glow, he stood. "Our hostess has informed me that all and sundry need to be up and about for greenery gathering early tomorrow... in the woods."

Without a word, Lily stumbled to her feet, but that arm stayed around her waist, righting her in the gloom.

The corridors to the chambers were narrow, as befitted an old manor house, and the thought of creaking floors and dark passages sent tremors scattering.

Mr Mereworth had been rather parsimonious with candles, keeping them locked away, and she had oft crept fearfully to bed, feeling her way along blurred stairs and lightless hallways, but she was a grown woman now for goodness' sake; she had investments and a delightful townhouse with beeswax candles in every room – she was not to be frightened by silly tales.

Truly, Jack was the very devil in no disguise whatsoever.

"May I escort you, Lily? If you are feeling a little…unsettled."

Glancing up, she met Asher's amused eyes. "Was this intended to scare us ladies? Because it worked," she said, noting Sir John still comforting Catherine. "Did you *gentlemen* cook this up at the inn?"

"Ah, astute, clever Lily. That is why I…"

He gazed down upon her and she waited for him to finish. He didn't. "Why you what?"

"Why I will escort you to your chamber and check for rabid hounds."

Lily was aware this was her chance to say no. To tell him she was not in any way unsettled. But his firm palm still branded her waist, and those fine eyes solemnly perused her.

And in truth she was terrified of the headless huntsman.

"Thank you. I would appreciate the gesture."

Most guests had hurried along in the cold corridors, but Lily ambled, watching as Asher tried to match her short stride. Finally, her corner chamber loomed, and she wasn't quite sure what to say or do.

Did she want to invite him in? Did she want to complete number eight with Asher? Did he want to come in? Should she–

"Lily. I would like to kiss you again but feel there is only a thirty per cent chance of success."

The cadence of her heart rumbled fast and loud as she leaned back against the door. "Why such low odds?"

"You told me to leave you alone the last time."

"I was…nervous." Fearful and overwhelmed were better words.

"And now?"

Fearful and overwhelmed still, but she hoped that was simply because of the grim ghost story. *Embrace all new adventures,* she told herself. "You would have to try again for me to know."

She thought he would smile, but his face remained stern as one arm reached to the side and he leaned close.

"Lily…" he whispered, his mouth moments away.

A violent shiver shook her as wind gusted through the gaps in the hall window, the pane rattling in its wobbly home.

"Perhaps," she whispered, "we should go inside. You can check for headless huntsmen as well."

Asher didn't take his contemplative eyes from her as he slowly nodded. She thought he'd leap at the chance, but he almost seemed reluctant.

Turning, she pushed the solid oak door and warmth rushed from the fire inside the chamber. Setting the candle lantern by the bed, she… Well, she wasn't sure what to do.

Often, late at night, she had wondered how the fulfilment of this item on her list would play out. She imagined laughing with her would-be lover, falling to the bed in a tipsy giggle, maybe even removing some clothes.

But Asher stood, looking serious. "Lily? What do you want?"

She stared. This is what she wanted. To have a man ask her what *she* wanted. And now she didn't know. Didn't know where to start.

"I want to kiss you," she finally said. Surely that would be the first piece of advice if a book entitled *How to Seduce a Rogue* existed.

A smile broke his serious features. "I can provide that." He strolled near and gently started removing the pins from her hair.

"Do you have a fondness for loose hair?" she mumbled.

"Only for yours. It's a crime to bundle it back, Lily. You looked beautiful tonight with it framing your face."

"Thank you. I…this year I am trying new things. I… invest in businesses, as you know. Shipping. And perfumed soap is particularly interesting and–"

A fingertip stopped her gabbling.

"I will indeed want to hear of every small fortune you make," he said, letting her hair tumble down, "but for now I need to comply with your request."

And with that, his lips lowered.

Asher only held one hand to the side of her head, and yet she felt him everywhere. Tingling shot from their lips to every limb, every inch of skin with exquisite agony.

Mr Mereworth's kiss had always been rather sloppy but she wouldn't think of that now, not when Asher was trailing his other hand around her waist and pulling her inextricably towards him.

Meeting his body with a bump, she gasped as his lips weren't the only thing firm.

This was her chance – to be the new Lily and forever banish the memories of Mr Mereworth, his wet mouth and pudgy fingers. To gain control over her life and desires.

She chased his kiss, pressing close, grasping with frantic hands, but feeling anxious and jittery all at the same time.

This was what she'd come here for. To complete her list at this Christmas gathering.

But the wind howled outside in evident displeasure, and that chased desire bled away to be replaced by fear and foolishness.

A vision of Mr Mereworth intruded, his sweaty face hovering, his ghostly white nightshirt smothering, and to banish the horror, she dragged Asher to the bed by his neckcloth. She nipped at his throat and slid her hands down his solid body.

All would be fine; passionate lovemaking was surely the answer, but a sob left her throat as his shirt refused to pull from his breeches, and where were the bloody buttons?

Strong hands suddenly grabbed those trembling fingers, and Asher panted into her neck for several moments, pressed his body hard against hers, and then hauled himself away.

"Lily," he said, voice hoarse and eyes direct. "What is it that you truly want?"

Lawks. Hadn't she made that obvious. "You."

"Why?" he asked, face shadowed.

"I…"

Without his warmth, the nervousness grew and spread. She had to complete number eight. To start her new life. To expel the ghosts forever. But none of that came out…

"Exactly, Lily." A gossamer kiss pressed her forehead and he clutched her close again. "When you know why it is you want me, then we will finish this." Pulling back, he cupped her chin. "I shall call your maid to prepare a hot drink and keep you company."

She shook her head, not wanting anyone and feeling sure he was merely making excuses. Maybe he didn't desire her after all – why should he? A cold widow with fumbling hands and a too-clever brain.

Asher strode to the door but looked back as his fingers grasped the handle.

"And so we are clear, Lily Mereworth, I want you desperately. I want you because you are beautiful, brave, sensual and so very clever." He stepped through before closing the door softly, leaving her to sink onto the bed.

Asher took himself to the bitter draught of the hall window, compelling his body to calm. He was so achingly aroused, so incredibly needing of Lily Mereworth, but if he had bedded her tonight, he had a feeling it would all go wrong in the morning.

He'd sensed a desperation within her, and it hadn't felt right. There'd been no…tenderness, and Lily's passion had felt forced.

A quick tup wasn't what he wanted. A quick tup followed by an embarrassed silence the next day.

Anxiety and confusion roiled within. Slightly lost, now he stood alone.

Damn it, he already knew he desired Lily, knew he harboured more tender sentiments, but he hadn't calculated the chances of that further inexplicable sensation arising.

And at this time, it appeared the chances of feeling that sensation were significantly higher than sixty per cent.

FUN IS NOT OVERRATED

Furtively keeping an eye on the blond woman tying ribbon around a bundle of twigs, Asher sidled up to Winterbourne.

"What have you found out?"

Using the Crown's resources in this way was probably unethical but Asher had given over twenty years to the service, so assumed a little leeway would be allowable.

Grinning, the marquess stamped his hocks in the bitter cold. "The servants of this house are terribly tight-lipped, but I did manage to talk with Rosalind's maid who also looks after Lily."

The chap blew on his raw red hands before a cunning smile split his lips. "Under my persuasive charm, she was very forthcoming and told me that Lily started a list last winter. Her late husband was a bit of a fatwit apparently, always criticising and berating her – mutton-headed oaf. Anyhow, her and Rosalind created this list of bold and spirited objectives for this year, and except for two, she's accomplished the lot – investing, staying out late and such forth. Did you know she even emptied Devilish

Dominic's pockets at his gaming hell? I'll have to rag him about that."

"Hmm. We know most of that already. The important question is what her number eight is that remains uncompleted?" Asher had a horrible idea he knew after last night.

"Oh. Er. Well, the maid wouldn't tell me."

"What! You said she fell for your charm."

"She did! That was all valuable information. One item on this list involved reading bawdy novels. I mean, how interesting is that?"

Asher glared and stooped to pick up the boughs of greenery that Lucas's mother had dumped at his feet.

FURTIVELY KEEPING an eye on the chocolate-haired man hefting a bunch of foliage, Lily sidled up to Rosalind.

"What have you found out?"

Earlier, Rosalind had revealed she had some interesting news, but the arrival of a screaming Alice had curtailed the conversation. Now they stood outside in the freezing forest, with their hostess bossing everybody about in relation to the cutting, collecting and distribution of greenery for the house.

The woods at Whittlebury weren't scary by day – no headless huntsman as yet and the only hound was a beagle called Sid, currently chasing his own tail. In fact, the forest appeared giving and restful, celebrating with them the eternal rite of winter.

Rosalind pursed her lips as Robert pummelled Billy's ankles with a rather large stick. "Well, it seems the Marquess of Winterbourne has been interrogating my maid for information about your list."

"No," she spluttered.

"Hmm, don't worry. Under my direction, she only told him the barest of details. Matilda had the best fun with the marquess. He flattered her with lines from Byron and whispered that her hair resembled an onyx night. I can quite see how the ladies fall for him."

"Bah! They're all scheming cheats," Lily ranted, trying not to watch as Asher bent over to pick up more vegetation.

"It does demonstrate his regard for you."

"Snooping about my past and list?"

"Wanting to know *you,* Lily. You can be quite…reticent about things."

Fighting with a bundle of holly that was thrown into her arms, she was unable to answer as Rosalind charged off in the direction of some hawthorn.

"Don't scratch yourself, Lily," a voice murmured, and the load lightened.

This morning, the sight of Asher compelled her breath to shorten and heart to thrash.

A rusty greatcoat adorned his person, its three capes lifting in the breeze. The exertions of wandering in the woods had caused a red flush to his high cheekbones and his hair was tousled and wild, hat lost to a branch.

Despite the manner in which they'd parted, his eyes twinkled, lips curving in a warm smile. White puffs of air escaped his mouth, and she wanted to capture them in her hands – a precious piece of Asher Rainham.

How could she have ever hesitated last night?

She blamed the ghost story – resurrecting the dead, their skeletal fingers touching her with dusty memories and raw unease, but with the detachment of day, she realised her need for him had nothing to do with Mr

Mereworth or number eight or even that Asher seemed to want her exactly as she was.

No, she didn't want him simply to fulfil some ridiculous list, but because he was mindful, handsome and kind…

"There's only a ten per cent chance of finding fresh mistletoe. Wrong trees," he muttered.

And because he came out with the oddest knowledge.

"Nasty parasitic plant it is. Saps the strength of orchard apples."

And was unfailingly plain-spoken, but it was that candour she admired. Her husband had covered his criticism with beguiling words, couched his reproach with sighing disappointment so that she had always felt so very guilty…guilty for just being herself.

"Asher?" she whispered.

"Hmm?"

But now was not the time: Stretton shrieked, brushing mud from his breeches whilst Lucas showed off his fencing skills with a branch. A grumpy Rosalind muttered at there being no juniper and Robert was halfway up a tree.

"Help me find some rosemary," she said, dumping the holly to the bare earth and taking his arm.

Asher couldn't remember a day when he'd had such…fun.

Lily Mereworth didn't seem to mind the fact that he jabbered on about odds. And equally, she made him laugh, gently berating him when he'd stacked the laurel in length order, but also agreeing with him that it would help with the foliage arrangements.

After last night, he'd worried that he'd made the wrong decision in leaving. That she hadn't heard his words and felt unwanted or thought him a rum cull, but it appeared the opposite had happened. She'd strolled with a lightness to her step and a smile on her succulent lips that took his breath away.

Ahead, the brick and timber Helmdon Court lay snug in the landscape, its beckoning warmth a pleasant sight after the morning spent tackling the flora of the woods. The decorating was to begin this afternoon and although some considered it unlucky to do so before Christmas Eve, a besieged Lucas had finally given in to Rosalind's demands.

"Are you helping with the trimming, Lily?" He stared down at her as she huddled in a delightful fur-lined hood. The deep-blue wool pelisse she wore complemented her pale complexion, although her eyes were anything but cold this day; instead, they sparkled with affection and pleasure.

"Yes, although I do have my entertainment to organise as well."

"Do you need help?"

She peeped a smile at him and his hand clenched in tandem with a curious anomalous skip in his chest.

"'Tis all sorted, thank you. I… I have had a wonderful day, Asher. I cannot remember a time when I have had such…fun."

Warmth seeped through his body and that odd chest skip happened again. Perhaps 'twas the cold, as a seizure of the heart was more prevalent in winter months. "I hear you emptied the pockets of a gaming hell owner. Surely that was fun?"

"No, it was more…vindicating. That I could do it. I felt triumph, but I am not sure it was fun."

"Would you go there again?"

"No, I do not believe so."

"Would you spend another day, such as this, with me?"

That skip stopped. In fact, he couldn't feel aught in his chest. Maybe he was dead.

Asher turned to gaze upon her, but unlike last night, she looked him in the eye, those glacial lakes clear and direct.

"I believe I would like that very much."

His heart restarted.

NOT ALL BOLD NEW IDEAS ARE SENSIBLE ONES

It appeared a curious green colour and Lily wasn't convinced she wanted to taste it after all.

She pottered around the drawing room, sorting out the glasses and ensuring there was plenty of sugar and fresh spring water.

Admittedly, some might consider a night of absinthe somewhat vulgar, but she could think of no better setting in which to complete number five on her list than in the cosiness of Helmdon Court with friends surrounding her.

This reception room had been the first to undergo Rosalind's decorating storm and it now resembled a verdant grotto. Boughs of greenery, pine cones and ribbon hung from every rail, mantel and picture, and although a few might say it was a little overblown, the scent of winter – fresh and sacred – weaved its way around her like ivy.

Lucas had grouched that his wife would prefer to slumber with the vegetation than him, but she'd looped willow around his neck and dragged him near for a light buss. Everyone was getting used to their hosts' close intimacy and guests now smiled rather than frowned at the impropriety. Even Stretton had grown more relaxed, allowing Catherine to at least speak with Sir John.

The atmosphere of ease and openness was catching.

"Lily?"

She twisted to see Jack peering around the door. "I'm not ready yet."

"Just to give you this." He pulled something silver from his jacket and her eyes widened in delight. Held in his hand was a true absinthe spoon. In the shape of a diamond, it had elaborate slots to allow water to drip over a sugar cube and join the absinthe in the glass below.

"Where? How?" she spluttered.

"I have my ways," he declared mysteriously. "Rule seven, lovey – always be prepared." And with that, he returned from whence he came.

Marvelling at the intricate silver workmanship, she placed it on the table. Initially, she had planned to use a simple dessert spoon and hope for the best, but this would complete the spectacle.

LILY CAUTIOUSLY TAPPED her glass with a fork to gather everyone's attention, as Rosalind had done. It felt awfully common and so very wayward, but it did work, quietening the room.

All at once, nerves overcame her as eyes focused in her direction, but Rosalind smiled encouragingly, Lucas grinned with foreknowledge and Jack flipped her a wink.

Asher sat with arms folded, long legs lounging and hooded eyes focused on her loose hair.

"Thank you, everybody. Firstly, I would like to express my gratitude to our hostess for a wonderful time thus far." A ripple of applause was acknowledged by said lady with a regal nod, the demeanour spoiled in part by a sprig of mistletoe wedged behind her ear.

"Now, as *some* of you seem to know" – Lily gave Jack a glare, but the rogue simply chortled – "Rosalind and I came up with a list last winter. I had become…set in my ways and we decided that a list of new experiences, to be completed this year, would be freeing."

Rosalind clapped, bless her.

"Thank you, dearest. I have been, to my surprise, rather successful with some endeavours." She blushed, feeling terribly forward at being so…forward.

"No surprise to me," Lucas bellowed. "I'm coming for a loan once Christmas is over and Rosalind has put us in the Fleet."

Lily flapped her shawl, unsure if he was teasing. "Anyhow, I would like to say thank you to everybody that has helped me this past year. And I'd be delighted if you could all assist me in completing a remaining item on my list. To celebrate a year of adventure and to future years of adventure. I have learned we should all be open to whatever comes our way, with acceptance and compassion in our hearts."

Cries of "Hear! Hear!" resounded.

"What else did you achieve, dear?" asked Lucas's mother.

"Oh, well. I'll tell you lat–"

"Tell us all, Lily," Catherine urged. "I would like to know as well."

"Oh." Lily nervously gulped. Surely they would think some things foolish, but perhaps the first step to her new bold life was not to care about others' censure and judgement. To believe in oneself. "I burned a book on etiquette and read…more useful literature."

Rosalind clapped enthusiastically again.

"For number three on my list, I beat a crowd of gentlemen at whist and then invested my substantial winnings in shipping and soap in order to produce an income of my own – which was number four. The returns have been most gratifying and beyond expectation."

"Well done, dear," Lucas's mother praised. "I'll have to talk to you about that as I have some money in tin mines that I wish to move."

Encouraged, she continued, "For numbers six and seven, I stayed out the entire night at a Mayfair ball and managed to waltz with a libertine."

"That wasn't me," bemoaned Jack. "Why wasn't that me?"

Guests laughed, and the atmosphere became so convivial and merry. Lady Sidlow replied that Jack had more than enough widows to keep amused, and Lily almost wanted to cry with pleasure at the welcoming cordiality.

Long ago Christmases had involved nervous silence with disparaging eyes, and no greenery had ornamented the house as it had been considered "plebeian". They'd played cards and she'd pretended to lose…

Tapping her glass again, she continued, "However, number five still remains outstanding – to drink new-fangled absinthe. One of Rosalind's contributions, so 'tis only fair I insist she join me. Indeed, I hope you will all join us in accomplishing this last item on my list."

Sounds of enthusiastic agreement rippled the room as the servants entered. The majority of the guests had eaten early after the rigours of the day, and so she had merely organised a light supper to complement the absinthe.

"Is *everything* completed on your list, Lily?" a deep voice murmured, startling her.

"I believe it is everything that I wish to complete as..." She gazed up at Asher. "I remembered, today, that the main aim of my resolutions was to be bold and not cowed by people or situations. And do you know, I was actually being cowed by my own list of all things." She laughed but it was true. "I am in control of my list, not the reverse, and I can cross items off, add them at will or burn the whole thing, just as I did to Miss Pikesworth last year."

"Lily Mereworth, you are the most–"

She never heard what she was because an enveloping hug from behind caught her unawares.

"Well done," congratulated Rosalind. "I wish we had a few more volumes of Miss Pukesworthy to burn as it's so cold. Now, show us how this absinthe works. I'm sure I'll be wanting lots of sugar."

ASHER STOOD to one side of the fireplace, watching Lily explain how the vivid green liquor was to be drunk. He'd partaken of the foul stuff back in '06 when passing through Pontarlier but would try another glass to be social and support Lily.

Whilst she'd held the audience rapt with her list of achievements, he'd felt the probability of falling in love rapidly climb and wondered at what point he would just admit it had happened anyway.

"Damnation, it looks more like Whittlebury woods in here than, well, Whittlebury woods," said Lucas, edging in front of the heat and peering at the scarlet-berried holly dripping over the mantel. "Did Rosalind denude the whole forest? We'll have squirrels and badgers at the door, trying to find their homes."

Asher smiled, and they watched in companionable silence as the ladies marvelled over the revolting stuff.

"And why not try English ale instead? I didn't fight so our women would go all agog over French sophisticated tastes."

"We are at peace now, Lucas."

"How long for?"

Asher kept quiet. He had odds for Napoleon making a move from his exile and it didn't look good.

"Asher?" Lucas shifted uneasily. "Can I ask your advice?"

"As long as it's not about women, I don't–"

"No, no." He raked a hand through his over-long, blond hair. "But you understand people and 'tis Robert. He's so... I don't know. The slightest admonishment sets him off, and he thinks we don't want him, that we are thinking of an excuse to get rid of him. He ignores Rosalind, fights with Billy, and scowls at me."

"Like a bear cub with a thorn in its paw?" Asher raised a brow.

"Hmm. He's such a bright little lad, but he's seen too much unpleasantness on the backstreets of London, has had to survive with nothing, and it's left him as close as an oyster."

"I'll have a think, Lucas. See if I can come up with any ideas, but small people are not my forte."

"Small, big... I'm not sure we are all that different."

"ONE MUST PLACE a lump of sugar on the slotted spoon and then pour over iced water. The water collects the sugar and drips through the holes. With luck, the absinthe underneath" – Lily heaved a sigh of relief as the green became a milky opalescent – "should react with the water and cause this, er...*louche*, I believe the French call it."

She peered at the cloudy glass in trepidation.

"*La louche*," she repeated, savouring the word.

"Well, my dear," prodded Lucas's mother. "Try it."

Lily sipped.

And shuddered.

And sipped again. Would it be polite to pull a face?

Her maid oft concocted a tonic to erase the bad odours from one's breath and it tasted somewhat like that. Except the tonic was expulsed afterwards and this...

"Well?" asked Rosalind with trembling excitement.

"It's very...herbal. Aniseed and grass."

"Do you like it?"

"It's different."

"Better than sherry? Surely it's better than sherry. Anything is better than sherry."

Lily shrugged. "I'm afraid I still prefer sherry, but it is... unique. Try some, everyone."

Most of the guests appeared to have more fun mixing the absinthe than actually drinking it, so where was it all going? Lily felt sure some of the potted plants adorning the room would still be feeling the effects tomorrow morning.

Jack assaulted the piano with enthusiasm whilst Lucas's mother sang along, and many of the gentlemen moved to whisky or brandy, but she and Rosalind still gamely quaffed the stuff with blithe abandon, adding more sugar as the evening wore on.

Guests became ever more raucous as the various beverages were steadily consumed, and Lily took herself to the side table for a nibble of roasted pigeon pie.

Attempting to spear a slice, the fork slipped from her fingers.

Gosh, she thought, glancing at the clock on the mantel, the hands shimmering at around midnight, it would seem she was a trifle intoxicated. Absinthe did grow on one.

Bed.

She would take supper to bed.

Mr Merewor– Lily stopped herself. No longer would she refer to her husband in that lofty pedestalled manner but neither did she want to use his given name...

Mr M had not allowed eating in the bedchamber, as he'd said it promoted slothful rats, or had that been slothful Lilys? She giggled, imagining night-attired rodents lounging about, complaining of crumbs in the bed.

Grasping the edge of the table, she stood and turned, stumbling over her own feet, but strong arms encircled her waist, and despite being in a crowded room, she let her forehead fall upon the strong chest in front of her.

Gracious.

Absinthe certainly lowered one's inhibitions. Next, she'd be suggesting that Asher accompany her to her bedchamber.

"Would you accompany me to my bedchamber?" She bit her lip and peered up. "I need someone to carry my plate." Did that help? Did that sound less...trollopy? She didn't think so.

"Only the plate?"

"Hmm. I must admit that liquor does seem over-strong and I had some sherry as well."

"Oh, Lily. I expect that didn't mix well. You may have a slight headache tomorrow."

"I feel stunningly superlative. But... I believe I've never been befuddled before – 'tis a most unusual feeling."

"Two sheets to the wind, Lily, I would say. But we are lucky as everyone's occupied by Stretton singing *May the King Live Forever*. We can sneak out via the library."

His arm crept around her waist and she leaned into it. "Remember the sherry," she prodded.

SOMETIMES IT'S HARD TO BE A GENTLEMAN...

Asher considered himself a gentleman.

Indeed, he'd always had a firm control over pleasures of the flesh. But then he had never before tried to lead a giggling Lily up an old wooden staircase after she'd consumed apparently four glasses of absinthe and three glasses of sherry.

Her hands wandered.

Not that he was complaining, but she was far too bosky to be taken advantage of, and he still wasn't sure of the reasoning behind her desire for him.

"Lily, your hand is on my…derrière."

"Arse."

"I beg your pardon."

"Not you," she said behind more muffled giggles. "Your…posterior. Arse. 'Tis a much better word. More…earthy."

"Very well, Lily. Your hand is on my arse."

"Hmm. And a nice firm arse it is too. Do you know, I rather like absinthe. Earlier, I was thinking it tasted like something my maid concocts, but now I feel so…free."

"I'll remind you of that tomorrow, as you have a high chance of waking up with the very devil of a head pain."

Lily suddenly jumped a few steps and then paused, swaying. Asher reached forward to stop her fall, but she turned, looping her arms around his neck and leaning her weight against him.

Perched on different steps, they were nearly of the same height, and every inch of him craved the soft pliancy of her body, but he resisted pulling her close. The scent of violets and herbs invaded his senses, but he resisted that sensual entwining fragrance too.

All may have been well, had she not laughed. That husky giggle, right in his ear. The breath of it quaked down his neck and landed precisely in his groin.

"What chance is it, Asher?" she whispered, lips to his lobe. "Tell me? Forty? Sixty?"

An uneasy feeling that she was mocking him caused a pall. That's what his brothers had done and back then he hadn't been savvy enough to realise. Only after their muffled hilarity had ceased had he twigged. He didn't mind teasing but…

"Lily, are you making sport of me?"

The hallway and stairs were fairly well lit, probably so guests didn't break their necks on the way to bed, and her face scrunched, nose wrinkling.

"Making… I don't understand."

"The numbers I come out with."

"But I like them."

"You do?"

"Yes." She brushed her lips over his cheek and met his mouth in a soft kiss. "It's so logical in an illogical world. I love the sense of them. I understand numbers, Asher. I like numbers – it's how I win at whist and choose investments.

You could count in my ear and I'd tremble with excitement."

Asher was sure a few people would say there was something slightly odd about that pronouncement, but those people could bugger off.

"Then I would say, Lily, that there is a nine in ten chance of you feeling a little off-colour tomorrow."

He could have sworn she quivered, and so without further ado, he kissed her, hard. After all, he was only so much of a gentleman.

Intoxicating fervour enveloped him, from scent to skin. Lily's mouth was warm and welcoming, tasting of aniseed and dry sherry, and he could have remained there forever, but at least six people a month died from falling down stairs in London, so he gently pulled away.

"We have to get to bed, Lil– No, I mean…I didn't mean…" But Lily was already careering up the staircase, laughing as she went.

He caught up as she fumbled with the handle outside her bedchamber.

It was like last night but not.

This evening she seemed so full of life and verve, not afraid or desperate. The alcohol had affected her, but it was more than that, he realised.

Tonight, as she'd made her speech, they'd all been witness to Lily Mereworth spreading her phoenix wings.

Forthwith, the door sprung open and she flung herself into the warmth. As he'd requested, the maid had laid out a jug of spiced milk, some bread, and an orange from Lucas's conservatory. A fire roared in the grate, causing the bedchamber to appear incredibly…intimate.

He poured a glass of milk and turned to hand it to Lily who stood by the mantelpiece. Her wicked lips smirked as she instead sipped from a small glass of sherry, and he noticed a brimming decanter on the chest of drawers.

Silhouetted against the flame, he could admire every curve of her luscious body behind that raspberry dress.

A book lay to the side and he idly picked it up, anything to distract himself from the fruit that hung temptingly in front of him.

LILY WAITED, attempting to sip demurely at the delicious sherry.

But it didn't take long for Asher to glance up, a twinkle in his eye. "*Memoirs of a woman of Pleasure*? Is this your nature book?"

"It's not mine, and anyhow, you knew," she accused, but nevertheless heat rose in her complexion.

"Only an inkling. And only because Lucas asked me if I knew who Fanny Hill was the other day."

"Well, you seem to recognise the book."

Placing it back on the table, he came to stand close. "'Kisses, squeezes, tender murmurs, all came into play, till our joys growing more turbulent and riotous threw us into a fond disorder...'"

Her already heated cheeks exploded and she couldn't blame the fire, only her translucent skin which betrayed every turmoil, every emotion.

Reordering her shawl, she peered at his long feet. "What a tremendous memory. Do you read often?"

"I enjoy most literature – from the light to the heavy, the comic to the serious."

"My late husband only allowed etiquette and household books. He didn't approve of novels." Lily brought a palm to her mouth. She'd never mentioned Mr M to anyone but Rosalind. Where had that come from?

Asher's hand stroked over her loose hair, starting at the crown of her head and making its way down the curls. Like a contented cat, she arched to the caress, bending her neck to his touch.

"Your husband was a damnable fool."

"He said he loved me."

"Did he? Then he should have let you read whatever you liked. Possession is not the same as love. What else did he disapprove of?"

"I was too noisy, my laugh too strident. I folded things incorrectly and I ate too quickly. I wore flashy silks and my hair... Well, it's so trollopy when loose."

"Oh, Lily. Your laugh hits my nether regions like a cannon. I adore loose hair and flashy silks if they are yours, and I really couldn't give a fu– *damn* if you never folded another linen ever again."

"I loved him at the beginning. I was so...lucky. My father was just a lawyer and–"

"No." He placed his hands over her shoulders. "*He* was the lucky one. Lucky that he got to touch your glorious hair and hear that husky laugh and see all your glorious skin."

"Well, he never saw much of that, what with nightshirts in the way."

"Nightshirts?"

"Hmm." Lily wanted to button her mouth. The trip up the stairs had in some ways sobered her mind, but her tongue seemed as loose as her coiffure. "My husband always wore a nightshirt in bed."

"Always, as in *always*?"

She nodded.

"Bloody hell," was all Asher said.

"And me as well," that loose mouth gabbled on.

"Bloody hell," he said again, louder. "Lily… Not all men are like that. You should be savoured, cherished, caressed…stripped."

"Stripped? Should I?"

"Undeniably. Divested of every single item of clothing. Entirely naked."

Her unbidden mouth liked that idea and continued its jabbering, "I've never actually seen a man's bare chest. A real one, I mean. I don't think paintings count."

Draining her glass occupied her tongue for mere moments and then she peered up. Asher's expression was in turn aghast, amused and…aroused?

With no more sherry to occupy her blabbermouth, it rattled on unabated, tongue slack enough for two sets of teeth. "I would like to see your chest, Asher. It always feels so firm."

She thought he'd turn tail and run, like last night, but instead he started shrugging off his tailcoat.

Goodness.

Her tongue finally stilled as she watched Viscount Asher Rainham undo his waistcoat, standing there in the middle of her delicate pink bedchamber, flicking the silk-covered buttons with nimble fingers.

"I think… Don't stop, but I need to sit down," she said as he peeled off the bottle-green silk. Then his gold cufflinks. Then his stickpin.

Lowering herself to the bed, she admired those strong hands as he began unravelling what seemed like yards of neckcloth material, and she couldn't contain the quiver of excitement as his throat was at last bared.

Asher was quite tanned, and she bit her tongue to halt

the small whimper that wanted to abscond when he then pulled the shirt from his breeches. She'd felt desire once upon a time for her handsome husband but it had quickly been subdued – it wasn't ladylike – and even then, never had it felt so…primitive. Asher's unveiling caused her to salivate like a lone wolf stalking a doe.

"Lily?"

"Yes?" she whispered, eyes wide.

"I'm not a young man any more."

"No," she murmured, imagining all that age-bronzed skin and years of built-up muscle.

"You married a young man with a young man's body."

She reluctantly peeped up. What was he wittering on about?

His expression gentled. "I've forty-three years."

"Oh!" She finally took his meaning and laughed, causing him to frown heavily.

Here she'd been positively panting at the very sight of him and he was worried about his…whatever.

Standing, and pausing to check the room didn't spin, she slowly drifted over to place a hand on his cheek and caress his stubbled jaw.

For some strange reason, which she wouldn't dwell on for now, the roughness aroused her yet more. What would it be like to wake with a man entirely naked except for his layer of stubble?

But as for his concerns…

"Asher, those lines by your eyes and streaks in your hair reflect your life – commanding and dashing. They make me shudder with desire. I can't imagine your body being any different, and at this very moment, a frisson of delicious joy is coursing through me. I…ache in quite an unladylike way."

His eyes flashed dark as he yanked the white linen shirt over his head.

"Oh my!"

Lily hadn't imagined it would be so sturdy and... substantial; dark hairs scattered over his chest and a few silvery scars slithered like snail tracks across his broad shoulders. He didn't have brawn like Lucas, but a wiry toughness that did extremely odd things to her insides. And she had thought the stubble was bad...

Reaching out a finger, she brushed his upper arm, where things bulged, and under her caress, they flexed. She trailed more fingers over hot skin to that luscious throat and then down across his chest, scratching her nails through the hair, loving the feel of his muscles contracting.

Both their gazes followed her hand as it trailed over his taut stomach, another scar dissecting her path, and then further down to that inviting line of hair that arrowed down to–

ASHER TRAPPED her hand under his. Alas, he was already maddened by her touch but any more and she'd unman him.

"Lily?"

"Magnificent," she whispered, and he was sorely tempted to release that hand and to hell with it, but he instead removed the seeking touch and kissed her palm.

"I should leave."

"Leave?" The look of disappointment was both adorable and gratifying. "Again?" she complained. "But why? Is it the sherry?"

"Pardon?"

"My husband wouldn't kiss me if I'd drunk sherry. He said it tasted horrible."

Asher wanted to resurrect Mr Bloody Mereworth solely so he could clout him one. What an utter cod's head.

Twisting, he bent down to place one hand behind Lily's legs, the other on her back, swinging her up into his arms.

"Oh!" she gasped. "No one's ever… Heavens, is this proper?"

After striding the two steps to the bed, he laid her upon it. He expected Lily to protest, but tiredness now etched itself upon her face in the lantern's flickering glow, and she remained supine, scrutinising his chest and arms with eyes wide.

The chinoiserie table clock displayed the hour as nigh on one, and refilling the glass, he supped her sherry, relishing the clean, dry taste before perching at her side.

Just one thing. Then he would leave.

Leaning close to her parted lips, he lightly kissed her. They both tasted of the pungent drink now and as she responded, he deepened the kiss, pressing harder, groaning as her finger traced patterns on his bare shoulders.

That was all he'd thought to do – to let her know he loved her sherry taste, but Lily twined her arms around his bare neck, dragged his body down to hers, plunging her tongue into his mouth and murmuring her delight.

Desire pulsed through him as her silk-covered breasts brushed his bare chest, and he shifted further onto the bed, covering her slight frame with his. He yearned to rip at her bodice, feel her nakedness, kiss her delicate skin. Fingernails scratched down his arm, causing a moan to escape his throat and hips to grind.

His hands scampered over her soft locks, twining them around his fingers. Then damn it, her legs slightly parted and his body fell into the void, making everything so much worse.

These past few days of wanting Lily Mereworth felt like a lifetime and had taken their toll. He ached for her.

It would be so easy, so easy to continue – to push up her skirts with tormenting fingers, to caress her core until she cried out, lick at her breasts, unbutton his fall, plunge into her heat.

To make her his.

But patience, his ever-fussy brain dictated.

Patience, he repeated to his groin.

Bugger off and stop ruining everything, that groin replied.

Yet he knew he must leave. The moment, once again, was wrong.

Lily was tired. He could feel it in her arms, now sluggish in their lingering touch. Not only that but the absinthe had lowered her defences, and he didn't want Lily in that way.

He wanted her thoroughly awake, completely aware, altogether naked and wholly desirous.

After tormenting himself with one last thrust of his errant groin, he brushed a gentle kiss upon her lips before drawing back. She moaned softly, and he memorised it, stashing it away.

Her arms dropped. "Asher?" she mumbled, eyes closing.

"I'll call the maid to assist you, but have no doubt that I adore your sherry. I adore your kiss and I adore…" A soft snore answered his adulation. "I adore you, Lily."

PAGAN RITES

"Lily, are you not…tired?"

"Not at all," she replied, cheerfully dabbing toast into her egg yolk. "In fact, I have never felt better."

Rosalind scowled and sipped black tea. "Do you not feel as though needles are stabbing your head? Or that your stomach has a whirligig in it? Or even that the sky is purposely gleaming white today, just to punish your eyes?"

"Er…no. I'm absolutely splendid, slept like a babe… Well, not the babe Alice as I heard her crying early this morning." She cut the sausage in half, the erupting aroma of sage causing her mouth to water. "But if it's any consolation, Rosalind, you won the absinthe night."

"If another bottle is the prize, you can keep it."

Lily patted her friend's hand and then returned to her breakfast, relishing the crispy bits on the edges of the bacon. "Since you feel so poorly, you can choose your prize."

Instantly, she regretted her offer as a sly look replaced the cropsick one on Rosalind's face.

Only the two of them sat breakfasting, as most of the guests were still abed, having retired exceedingly late after singing songs, playing games and generally drinking far too much until the early hours.

Her own evening now appeared a vivid fancy in the soberness of the breakfast room. Had one really asked a viscount to disrobe? Had he really kissed her with sherry on his lips? It all seemed more than a little debauched when one thought upon it, and her stomach squirmed with delight, skin flushing.

But then he'd left...again.

Asher was *so* much of a gentleman but if he didn't stop being one soon, she'd burst afire.

Lily shut her mind to where it all might lead.

Embrace new adventures, she would repeat to herself when fear lodged in her throat.

In Asher's company, she forgot all anxieties, enjoying his easy manner and attentive ways. But waking this morning, alone, qualms had indeed crept in.

If he wanted more, could she give it? Her heart was opening up; she could feel it cracking wide like a chick from an egg, but they hadn't long ago met, and did she really know this man?

"Yule log."

"What?" Lily shook her head and pushed the black pudding to one side – even her new bold self wasn't that brave.

"You can organise the collection of the yule log today. I'm supposed to do it, but I'm not sure I have the wherewithal. So much...brightness."

"But..." Lily gawped, her fork hovering over the mushrooms fried in butter. "I don't know how. We never had a yule log in Cheshire, and before that I always lived in townhouses with fireplaces too small for such tomfoolery."

"Well, I would love one and it has already been cut. I told Lucas it was traditional for it to be *freshly* chopped, but he complained it would smoke the house out, despite it being ash. It's been drying in the woods."

"But…"

"I'll give you a map. You can walk from here with the stable boys. They have chains, horses and suchlike to carry it. I also noticed some juniper near there so you can collect that as well."

"But…"

"And it has to be today as the weather's going to turn. The log can go in the stables till we light it tomorrow."

"But…"

"Thank you, Lily. I've hardly seen Alice with all the organising to do." And Rosalind bussed Lily's forehead before she left, trailing rose perfume in her wake.

"But…"

ASHER WATCHED from the courtyard as Lily flapped her arms in the cold and glared at a smirking, bulky stable master. She appeared to be wearing the entire contents of her wardrobe this morning. Hat, shawl, mittens, muff, redingote, cloak and if he wasn't mistaken a strange furry item over her ears – the entire ensemble a deep amethyst.

"You don't really need me, do you?" she groused to the stable master.

"Might be sommit. Yer never know," the fellow replied. "And I can't read maps too well. 'Twas autumn when we cut the tree. All looks a mite different in winter."

At nine this morning, a grinning Lucas had prodded Asher from a blissful dream – something to do with a certain luscious blonde in a bath of sherry. Lucas had requested his help with the yule log, but the sly bugger hadn't mentioned Lily was organising it, although by the adorably grumpy look on her face, she felt rather irritable about it too.

No question, it was cold enough to freeze the ballocks off a cat today. The sky emitted a strange light – opalescent and shimmery – but at least it was dry and without any wind to whip the skin.

"Good morning, Lily," he called, striding towards her, and pleasure coursed through his body at her look of gladness.

"Asher. I hope you know something of yule logs, because I am at a loss."

"Er. No, actually, always lived in the City."

"Oh, me too. Maps?"

"Those I can do. In fact, I helped John Cary with his Hampshire map – two and a half miles to an inch accurate." A true fact, but Asher promptly worried that sounded boastful. Surveying had always come easy to him and indeed, part of his youth in the Intelligence Service had been spent mapping land in enemy territory…and being shot at, but that was another story.

Lily handed him a creased bit of paper. Unfolding it, he found odd squiggles, a few lines, some squirrels, the Prince Regent's throne and what looked like a cow with arrows adorning it. He rotated the map. It didn't help.

"Is this all we have? Is there some kind of key?"

"Rosalind drew it. The squiggles are trees and the lines the path."

"And the cow?" He pointed.

"Oh. I don't know."

Asher attempted to stimulate his cold brain. Was the cow a codeword for yule log – its milk the life-giving liquid of nature? Or the arrows a clue as to the undulation of the land?

An abrupt smell of leather and horses pervaded the air as the stable master leaned over, also breathing an ale wind in their direction. "Thas the cow kept in a paddock by the east woods."

"Why is it sprouting arrows?"

Incredulity wrinkled the man's features. "'Cos it's Farmer Fletcher's cow."

He pottered off, muttering about town folk, and Asher contemplated the map again. "I think this could take some time."

Previously, Lily had never enjoyed walking in the woods, it being more of a Rosalind trait, but she had to admit that strolling along with Asher was an absolute pleasure.

Once, she and Mr M had picnicked on Box Hill, but he'd complained about the sandwiches not having enough cucumber, demanded that Lily read to him as nature was tedious, and had whined that sitting on the ground was simply common.

She tried not to compare the two men, but… Asher didn't feel the need to fill the silence with pointless chatter and equally didn't require her to amuse him with stories. Instead, they both listened to the sounds of the woods and, for the first time, she understood Rosalind's love of it.

A few brave robins chattered to each other on the bare branches, and a light breeze sprang up, causing the trees to groan and creak in displeasure.

Behind them, the horses dragged dangling chains, whilst the stable boys laughed and chatted about the upcoming Christmas feast and which maids they'd managed to kiss under the mistletoe.

It was all so agreeable, and a warmness filled her very soul.

Imagine if every Christmas was like this. Gathering greenery. Decorating the house. Walking the woods or the London streets. All with Asher by her side.

Oh, she had no doubt she would have to share him with the Government, as Lucas had mentioned his hours were often long and arduous, but that didn't bother her in the least. She had her own business to attend to, her own affairs to run.

But imagine after a long day working… When he came home.

Maybe they would have a light supper together. Some wine. Talk of their day, its trials and tribulations. Perhaps they would bathe together – she'd always wanted to do that. Then they'd retire abed. Asher would trail those long fingers over her entirely unclothed figure, kiss her mouth, tasting of sherry, and then he'd cover her body with his. Naked skin to naked skin, sliding and–

"Your breathing is strained, Lily. Are we going too fast? I didn't think to ask how you felt this morning after last night's absinthe. You appeared so sprightly."

"I am quite well. Wearing too many layers, I believe, for these exertions." *Or thoughts.* But she'd better keep that to herself. "And I'm afraid your odds were slightly flawed last night concerning my overindulgence as I feel marvellous this morning. I must be your one in ten."

He stopped abruptly to gaze at her and raised his hand as if to cup her cheek, but a lad's snigger caused it to drop. "No, Lily, I do believe you are my one in a hundred."

Smiling, unsure what he meant, she walked on.

"THERE IT BE," shouted the stable master.

And indeed, there it was.

A huge chunk of tree that would only fit in the most enormous of fireplaces. Luckily, Helmdon Court had those aplenty; in fact, Lily felt sure a whole family could fit in its inglenook…with room to rent.

Whilst Asher helped attach the shackles, Lily could only admire his broad shoulders as he removed his greatcoat and jacket. Dirt grazed his buckskins but it didn't seem to bother him, nor did the weight as he raised the log for the chains to be attached.

Certainly, he'd lifted her to the bed last night with nary a gasp.

She wondered what else he did to keep so trim – sword fighting obviously, horse riding probably and maybe boxing, stripped to the waist and–

"Lily? Come sit atop the yule log. Ryan here says it's good luck to be the first."

"Oh! Thank you." She stepped up and peered at the huge log wrapped in chains; it resembled a trussed-up boar, ready to break free at a moment's inattention. Her favourite cloak would get muddy and her maid would complain, but to blazes with it. She was now wild and free and open to all adventures, even soggy ones.

"Give 'er a seat," prompted the stable master. "Can't have a lady getting a wet ar–" He scratched his head. "Er, backside."

"Seat?" queried Asher, frowning.

A wink from the roguish Ryan and his brow suddenly cleared, but she was still at a loss.

Asher stood in front of the log and patted his knee. "Come sit, Lily. *Together* we'll be first."

Gracious! How very wicked. A man's lap? Surrounded by grinning boys and a leering stable master?

Tentatively, she turned and capable hands grabbed around her waist, pulling her to his warm lap. Arms enfolded her and despite the indecent public display, she sank into his chest, firm thighs and strong arms.

"Well I never, lookie there," Ryan said, pointing to a cherubic-looking lad. "Dave's found some mistletoe." And he wafted it over their heads.

Never before had she felt so…immoral. And yet what an agreeable feeling.

She was sitting in a man's lap, in the middle of the woods – he wasn't even wearing a jacket – and she was going to kiss him.

Their lips didn't meet for long, the catcalls and jeering saw to that, but despite the audience, she'd never experienced anything so intimate. It all suggested something rather pagan, like some woodland winter ritual.

"Stop wiggling, Lily," whispered Asher into her ear, and she gulped at the heat in his hazel eyes.

"Righty ho," bellowed Ryan. "Lads, get this log back to the stables sharpish and there's a pint in it for each of yer. Sky's looking downright murky."

The pagan fairy tale ended abruptly as the horses jerked into motion, nearly throwing them to the ground. Ryan and his cohorts tramped off towards Helmdon, the yule log gouging a path through the forest.

"I have been instructed to find some juniper before we can return," Lily bemoaned.

"Juniper? In the woods? Are you sure?" Asher questioned. "I thought it more a heathland plant."

"Hmm. On the map, those grey scrawls."

"Not squirrels then?"

"Rosalind does know her plants."

Asher shrugged but donned his strewn coat and they headed for the fabled squirrel land.

THE SKY no longer looked downright murky – it *was* downright murky.

Leaden clouds loomed as far as Asher's eye could see, as though lowering, ready to crash upon their heads at any moment.

"I think we need to turn back, Lily."

"But the map says it's near this arrow."

Looking at the crumpled paper again, Asher was now sure that the grey scrawls were in fact squirrels and not juniper at all, but the forest had fallen deathly quiet, all creatures having retired to their earthly homes.

If he'd been in France, he would have weighed up the possibility of an enemy ambush. As it was, he calculated only a three in ten chance of getting home without some kind of mishap.

"We'll come back tomorrow."

From the map, he'd worked out a shorter route home via the Prince Regent's throne drawn in the left corner. It was nearly midday by his fob watch and having wandered further into the woods, it would now be at least an hour back to Helmdon Court.

"I suppose." Lily sighed. "Although you will be busy organising your entertainment."

Damn.

Asher swallowed. He *always* remembered things.

Indisputably.

He knew every date of every battle in the whole damn war, recalled every man's name who worked for him, and even identified the timings of Prinny's change of waistcoat.

Yet he'd forgotten about his entertainment.

Damn, blast and bugger.

He'd be like Lucas, hopelessly prowling the house and begging for ideas. It was all this pretty minx's fault. Lily stole his wits and...did things to his body and heart and brain. "I think the juniper is a lost cause, but I'm positive I'll have time to return on the morrow."

Surely, he would; how long could one spend organising an entertainment for blazes' sake? He'd detailed the reconnaissance mission for the Second Battle of Porto in two hours.

"Very well." She skipped towards him, looking rosy-cheeked and rosy-nosed.

Touching her glowing skin, he opened his mouth to utter the words "it might snow" when a white flake fluttered down between them.

"Oh, how pretty," Lily whispered, but Asher wasn't thinking about that; he was looking up.

A severe pallid sky glowered back down, blocking light and giving the forest an ominous air.

Another pristine fleck fell, and as though beckoning its friends with a *come along, there's plenty of room down here,* a flurry descended.

"Oh, that's a little more concerning," muttered Lily, and he could only concur.

Why hadn't he weighed up the odds of snow? Too bloody occupied with thoughts of Lily's backside in his lap, that's why.

"We must hurry back to Helmdon or find shelter."

They walked quickly, but the flakes multiplied, concealing the floor in a sugar dust that made it difficult to see the lie of the land.

A covering overlaid Lily's cloak and any other time he would have romantically said she resembled a comely ice sculpture, but he was aware she might become a permanent one if they didn't find refuge.

"What's that?" Lily queried as something square emerged from the gloom.

He peered forth and recognised the shape instantly.

"Well I never," he declared. "That's the Prince Regent's throne."

HOW VERY IMPROPER

Logs. A bottle of something murky. Blankets that smelled of horse. A pair of old boots. An inferior-quality shepherd's crook.

Pottering around the small woodsman's hut, Asher catalogued other items for potential use whilst Lily shook off her damp cloak and redingote and stood shivering in the middle of the…hardly a hut, more of a hovel.

Still, at least it was dry, and he shrugged off his greatcoat, hunkering down to stack logs and some kindling in the small grate.

"There's no tinderbox," Lily said, searching along the mantel. "We'll freeze. Perhaps we should try for Helmdon."

"I have…"

Asher rummaged around in his greatcoat – so voluminous it could have hidden a picnic. Instead, he produced two pieces of gingerbread wrapped in cloth, a flint, his knife and some touchpaper.

"That's very fortuitous. Did you rate our odds of getting stranded that highly?" Lily smiled.

"I nearly froze one night in the Spanish countryside

without means of a fire and since then... Well, old habits die hard, it seems."

Crouching, he struck the back of the knife with his flint, attempting to light the thin paper. Soaked in saltpetre, it should have ignited easily, but it felt slightly damp.

"Do you think it will snow for long?" asked Lily, gazing out the one very small window. Someone had stuffed cloth around the edges to keep out the draught and it was grimy as hell, but at least it gave some view to the outside world.

"From my knowledge of midday snow in this part of Northamptonshire, it should cease after a few hours. For long enough to get back to Helmdon anyhow.

"Eugh."

Glancing back, he found Lily now sniffing the bottle of something murky.

She scrunched her nose. "Smells like...autumn."

A spark finally lit the touchpaper and the kindling flamed, producing smoke that curled up the chimney and thankfully didn't return. "I worried it may be blocked. There's a tw–"

Lily's amethyst skirts came to stand in front of him, fingers holding the murky bottle. "What's this?" she asked, waving it in front of his nose.

When he'd first entered the hut, his only thought had been to secure the building and gain warmth for them both. Now, kneeling on the floor, with Lily's perfume permeating the room and her wool skirts brushing his face, his skin prickled with the intimacy, throat tightening.

He coughed and stood.

She smiled and winked.

Taking the bottle from her fingers, he sampled the

murky liquid, fully aware of the chances of poisoning. "Beech rotgut."

"Beech?" She wrinkled her nose.

"It's actually very nice. They ferment the young leaves with other herbs of spring. Try some. It's better than absinthe, less bitter."

"Hmm. I am open to new adventures, but beech liquor may be going a smidgen too far." Cautiously, she sipped. "Tastes like…mouldy rugs."

"It keeps well and there's a three–" He cut himself off, aware he was blabbering.

"So," Lily said, "what do we do now? You must have been in situations like this before?"

"Er. Lucas and I once got caught out in a fierce storm near Vimeiro."

The logs collapsed in the grate, startling him, and a sense of disappointment leached throughout as Lily meandered away. That disappointment soon turned to satisfaction as she perched on the edge of a small bed…an item he hadn't initially catalogued as being potentially useful. She sipped more beech rotgut and licked her lips…slowly.

The minx.

"And what did you do to pass the time?"

"Lucas had been shot in the leg, so I had to dig out the bullet – with a rusty knife."

Asher wanted to silence his own tongue with a rusty knife. What a senseless thing to say to a lady.

"Poor Lucas." But a curve lifted her lips, warmth lighting those ice-blue eyes.

Clearing his throat again, Asher took the two steps to where she was sitting. "I'd never before heard half the curses that spewed from his mouth that day."

"I have been practising curses as part of my new bold persona."

"Is it going well?"

"Yes, but only in the mirror. I say 'Damn, I hate brown' or 'Damn, why can't I say damn in company.'" He smiled but jolted as warm fingers found his hand hanging by his side. "Or sometimes I say 'Damn… I want Lord Asher Rainham.'"

Longing poured through him at those softly spoken words, and he entwined his fingers with hers. She stared at their merged hands, only presenting his eyes with her bowed head.

"Why the 'damn' though?" he asked, kneeling on the grubby floor in front of her.

Lily didn't answer, simply rubbed his fingers.

Aware of her reticence, he pulled his hands from her clasp and placed them on her knees. He trailed fingers up the woollen skirt covering her thighs, heard a hitch of breath, and then laced them around her waist.

Leaning close, he whispered in her ear, "Why the 'damn', Lily?"

"I… It wasn't supposed to be like this."

"Are you talking about number eight?"

"In some ways, yes. In some ways, no. My number eight was to seduce a rogue."

Asher solely nodded. He'd known it was something like that, although he hadn't realised he fell into the rogue category; his men would laugh their hessians off.

"But… You… I…"

"Shall I begin instead, Lily Mereworth?" He kissed her mouth, a light peck. "I adore you." Startled eyes met his, the amber flame of the fire reflected in sky blue. "I want a future with you. I adore everything about you."

"I bite my nails."

He picked up a delicate hand, and indeed the poor ends had been chewed to the quick. Kissing the beleaguered stubs, Asher leaned yet closer, forcing her legs to part and accept his body until they were flush.

"I say again, I adore you."

"But… I never wanted… I can't… To give myself, my very soul again, I–"

"I don't want to take your soul, Lily." He kissed her eyelids, tasting pure air and violets. "That stuff belongs to the verses of poets. But I do want to love it. I want to love you. The real you. Just as you are – spirited and shrewd. I wouldn't care if you chewed your toenails."

"Bleugh!" She nibbled her lip, not meeting his gaze. "But I don't know if I can be…"

"I know, Lily. I know you have been hurt and require further time to feel more for me, but as I said in your bedchamber, there is only one thing I need to know for now. Why? Why do you damn well want me?"

A smile finally appeared, and a smooth hand cupped his cheek. "I want you because you are understanding, kind and you'd risk your life for a friend. You…listen and hear and defend without being overbearing." The smile turned impish. "You are a worthy opponent at cards and I… I desire you. I want to feel those long fingers of yours brushing over my body, I want to feel your lips against my skin, I want your–"

Lily didn't get any further with her wants as her mouth was crushed beneath Asher's.

Firm and commanding, and she kissed him back,

opening to the onslaught and his smothered curse of pleasure.

But still doubts assailed her. "Asher?" she mumbled as he kissed his way down her throat. "You are a viscount."

"Hmm, yes." A nip on the sensitive bit under her ear nearly undid her, but she knew if she made love with Asher now, there'd be no going back.

He may let her retain her soul, but her heart would be his.

"A viscount with responsibilities. To your future lineage. An aristocrat. You could have any woman you wanted. A younger woman. Have heirs. I don't know if I can–"

He reared with an expression she hadn't seen before. As though she'd asked him to hang curtains.

"I adore you, Lily, but stop spouting nonsense. For a start, my father, and in fact my entire family are valets. Your lineage is no doubt more noble than mine. I was only given the viscountcy for saving a jug-bitten duke who couldn't tell claret from arsenic."

Lily chuckled. It was so like him to downplay his talents, as though saving lives was a normal thing to do on a rainy Wednesday afternoon.

"But now you have responsibility."

"To be happy, yes. We all have that responsibility to ourselves and others. Our time in this world is short, and I have never known or understood this concept of love before. I care for my family and the people I command but this…this feeling I have for you is not to be given up for responsibility, a conceited view of my title or even a future heir. I am no young cub, Lily. I have two score and three." He gazed down at her fiercely. "And I know exactly what I want. I want you."

Such declaration of intent caused her breath to catch and her heart to painfully pound. The reaction of her fingers was more primordial; they yearned to wrest every item of clothing from his wiry frame.

"Asher. I do believe I adore you also."

"Why don't we…" He touched that sensitive ear bit again – the beast. "Why don't we show our adoration for each other then?"

Lily felt like a young girl again. Afraid and yet not. Excited and shivery because this was Asher and she remembered his words from the previous night.

"I want to be cherished, caressed and…stripped," she said, and then blushed – how improperly demanding.

Wrinkles creased Asher's eyes in tandem with his smile. This close, she could see today's stubble on his jaw, a lone grey hair in his eyebrow, a tinge of red on his high cheekbones and the way his eyes now gleamed hazel green at her words.

Leaning forward, she kissed him, and they fell into adoration together. No lists or games, just mutual want and desire as she tugged his mouth to hers and fell back onto the lumpy bed, dragging Asher with her.

It wasn't really a bed, more a plank on legs; things pressed in her posterior and it creaked rather worryingly, but none of that mattered because Asher was adoring her neck, throat and lips, murmuring praise.

There was no better place to be.

His murmuring grew to muttering as her sleeves proved stubborn, and he raised up.

"I think we will start with the stripping," he growled.

"How…shocking," she managed before being swiftly turned and having her buttons attacked. Asher's fingers proved nimble indeed, unthreading her laces with a steady hand, and at last some skin must have shown as a kiss landed on her naked shoulder.

More pulling and pushing of material, tabs and ribbons and she thought maybe there was after all something to be said for nightshirts – straight over the head with no fuss. But then she would miss the occasional caress of a hand along her sensitive back, the touch of breath at her bare nape, the rustle of material as it slivered down her skin.

"Turn over, Lily," his voice rasped, but suddenly nerves, akin to Asher's own the previous night, overcame her.

"I'm... I'm not young any more, Asher. I have...wrinkles."

Obviously he wasn't listening. "Hmm. Perfect," he hummed.

But still she didn't turn.

Asher brought his weight to rest on her back and she could feel every solid inch of his body – shirted chest abrading her naked spine, mouth at her bare shoulder.

"Lily, if you don't turn over, I shall make love to you like this." His words were accompanied by a firm shove of hips, and she gasped at the inflexible press of his arousal.

Most intrigued, she thought about staying exactly where she was, but eager to see as well as feel, and not caring about wrinkles in the slightest any more, she turned, only to become twisted up in petticoats and chemise. Growling at the scads of material, she sat up, impatient, and tore at the silly wool dress that prevented her from feeling his touch.

ASHER DIDN'T THINK his aching need could grow any stronger, but then Lily raised onto her knees and yanked at her clothing, tearing the bodice. The stays were flung across the room and the chemise dragged from her body until she kneeled in all her naked glory, shoulders straight, blond hair flowing about her, delicate pink nipples peeking through the long strands.

Venus came to mind – rising from the blankets, lush and brazen, her skin so pale, so translucent that it shimmered alabastrine.

Gently, he kissed her throat, felt her swallow against his lips as her hands rose to clench at his shoulder, and he dragged his mouth lower.

He couldn't fathom her concern over wrinkles – all he saw was feminine grace and beauty.

Lily was perfection.

"Oh! Ash," she whispered, and he had to force himself to breathe, to slow, when all he wanted to do was pounce on her.

"I love it when you say that," he murmured, beguiled by her soft skin.

The fire spat and popped, bringing him to his senses, and quickly he unbuttoned his waistcoat, tore at his neckcloth. Lily joined in the frenzied undressing and she leaned forward to unlace his shirt.

Her fingers slid to his waist, pulling at the material, brushing his groin, and a moan left his throat.

The damned minx did it again, a teasing smile on her lips.

Slanting, he kissed her breast, laving the pretty pink crest. That soon halted her seeking hands and instead they clutched at his hair, tugging and demanding.

Now nothing seemed frenzied enough, and with the shirt wrenched over his head, her hands caressed his chest. He had to turn to remove his bloody boots, but Lily didn't sit back. She kissed his shoulders, nape, spine, the burn scar on his upper arm.

Standing, he tugged his breeches off and Lily... Lily stared.

He'd forgotten. He'd forgotten that if she'd never seen a man's chest previously, it was highly likely she'd never seen a fully naked man before either. In a high state of arousal. Very high.

"Lily?"

She reached out a hand and caressed his stomach. He suffered her touch and thought to calculate the odds of the bed collapsing, desperate to calm his pulse.

"It's all so very...virile," she said, and her wandering fingers lowered.

That was it.

Enough was enough, and he grabbed her hand, pushed her back against the rough blanket, covered her slight frame with his and kissed with ruthless craving.

He was supposed to cherish, but pent-up ardour brought out the animal in them both. Lily nipped at his neck, so he devoured her breast. Slender legs had already parted to accept his weight, and his fingers smoothed over her ribs and soft stomach until reaching the blond curls guarding her womanhood.

Lily jolted beneath him as he stroked, breath catching and a cry resulting as he lapped her breast at the same time. To his knowledge, it had been some while for Lily too and although she was no maiden, he needed her ready and wanting.

"Asher," she cried, "I dreamed of you touching me."

He snarled, that was the only word for it. He wanted to do everything she'd ever dreamed of.

"What else? What else do you want?"

She shook her head, bucking against the palm of his hand, the pleasure nearly upon her.

"What else do you want? How do you want me?"

Glazed blue eyes opened to his. "I want…"

And Asher knew. He knew her desires, her need. She wanted to be in control. To be bold and freed.

Removing his hand, he grabbed hold of her arse and flipped them both.

A sharply drawn breath was her answer as his beloved found herself sprawled over his body, legs straddling his hips.

She levered herself up, hands pressed against his chest, blond hair falling about their bodies. Fisting some in his hand, he lifted to kiss her fiercely. "Take me, Lily. My phoenix. Burn me with your fire and life."

With intrepid fingers, Lily stroked over his torso and down his stomach. He thrust up under her touch, feeling her heat, and then soft steady hands caressed him, guiding him in.

Asher tried to think of cold snow, of how long the beech liquor would last, anything to stave off the soul-searing rapture as Lily slid down onto his body.

Taking. Conquering. Surrendering. Tightness and heat gripping him.

HE FILLED HER – they were the only words.

Constricted pleasure thrummed throughout Lily's body and she couldn't seem to move. Asher's teeth were gritted, his hands clutching at her hips, neither demanding nor yielding.

Slowly, she shifted, lifted and sank, heard Asher gasp and her own wanton moan. She had to cry his name, not only with the pleasure but with the freedom and naturalness of it all.

Stirring and undulating, a rhythm established, a pulsing dance of carnality.

Hands roamed, bodies arched and mouths exchanged breathless kisses. Asher wasn't a noisy lover but that didn't mean she couldn't tell his desire – his fingers gripped, hips bucked, eyes glassy.

Faster. Rougher. And Asher's hands suddenly tightened on her buttocks, drew her down fiercely, just as he ground his own pelvis up, and she fell atop him, breasts grazing his chest. In that moment, ecstasy such as she had never known pulsed, climbed, soared through her body, and she cried out, shuddering in rapture.

Her mind blanked, limbs loose, voice hoarse.

Vaguely, she heard her name groaned, low and raw, and thought Asher must have taken his pleasure also, but without warning she found herself flipped onto her back, legs tangled around his hips as he caught her wrist and pounded into her, the bed hitting the wall with force.

She'd thought her rhythm had been wild, but it was nothing compared to her lover's. He yanked at her thigh, tugged it higher, dragging out the pleasure until her head spun.

No longer did Asher remain quiet. Harsh moans heaved from his throat until with a stifled roar, he threw his head back, body pulsing and rigid all at the same time.

Their limbs collapsed, panting and quivering, Asher's head against her breast, and blearily she wondered if it was always like this – so primitive, so *very* necessary. Never had she felt such passion.

It took some while for their lungs to fill, to slow the soft touches and warm kisses.

"Forgive me," Asher whispered. "I could have been more tender, more considerate, but I do believe I have been waiting my whole life for you and need overcame me."

She couldn't help the tear that fell, what precious words.

"I craved you as well, Asher. It was perfect." And she saw his concern melt to a smile in the glow of the fire.

"Rest now, my phoenix. It's still snowing, and we don't want your flame ever doused."

LADIES SHOULD USE APPROPRIATE LANGUAGE AT ALL TIMES. (MISS PIKESWORTH)

"You damn sod," Lily yelped, laughing and shaking the snow from her hood before gathering more from a thick branch.

"Now, now, Mrs Mereworth. Language. Simply because we are passionate lovers is no reason to–"

A clod crashed into the back of his nape.

"Ah ha!" she crowed in delight as he shivered, wetness trailing an icy path down his spine.

"I'm coming for you, Lily," he growled as she sprinted away to collect more snow.

Only two inches or so claimed the ground, enough for a snowball, but not to impede their progress, and he'd never felt happier than on this walk back to Helmdon Court.

Although aware Lily needed time, he felt sure they could have a future together.

Maybe he'd have to buy some curtains…and not work until gone midnight…and not comment on the chances of Napoleon escaping his island imprisonment every morning.

Another snowball sailed over his head as the manor

house came into view. It was almost on the hour of three, and he hoped the household hadn't been too worried about them. They'd managed to reassemble their clothing to some degree although that had been interrupted by Lily's wandering hands, and then…

His groin tightened despite the cold.

"Look, Asher, riders out searching for us."

They both hastened their stride as the horses approached, Lucas leading the small pack of men.

"Lucas," he shouted. "Sorry to put you out. We are–"

"Our Robert has run away."

Asher held the bridle whilst Lucas slid from his gelding.

"How long?" was all Asher asked.

"At least an hour."

"Could he have gone sledging?" Lily interrupted. "Or be with the village boys?"

Grimly, Lucas shook his head. "He's taken a saddlebag with food and clothing, and Rosalind's gold necklace is missing. The maid heard an argument 'tween him and bloody Stretton and he's fled. We are into the woods hunting, and Winterbourne is leading the search in the village."

"We'll get back to the house for more clothing," Asher said, "and then where do you want us? This is your patch."

"I've left maps in my study for you as I need your clever brains. Where would you go? It's Christmas, there are no stagecoaches, 'tis nearly dark, and Rosalind says we'll be knee-deep in snow by tomorrow."

"Caves? Abandoned buildings? We'll take a look at the maps."

"Thank you." Lucas said, remounting his Goliath of a horse.

"None needed. Go. Go find your boy."

"I SHOULD HAVE KNOWN," Rosalind fretted. "Why didn't I see it coming?"

Lily patted her hand. "You are not *all*-knowing, dear," she said, as her friend sat, wrinkling a handkerchief. "Do you know the reasoning behind his disappearance?"

"That cur Stretton. Apparently, he was waffling on to Lady Sidlow when Robert crashed into him and knocked him on his arse – made him look a fool." Rosalind's eyes narrowed and the handkerchief tore. "He grabbed hold of Robert's ear, called him an ignorant bastard, and told him the sooner we sent him away to school the better as a thrashing was just what Robert needed."

"Oh no. But you're not sending him away, are you?"

"Of course not. School, yes, but only the local village one. It's half a mile, for three hours a morning, not Eton. We wouldn't dream of sending Robert anywhere – he's so…hard yet brittle. He needs a stable home and we have tried to cosset him, but he… He won't accept us."

"Does he have any friends he may go to?"

Rosalind shook her head. "In London, he belonged to a wiper's gang, but here… No, he only seems to have sparring partners in the village." Abruptly, she stood to pace the rug in front of the fireplace. "I can't bear sitting around. I'll go searching in the woods."

"Take a footman," Lily yelled to her retreating back. "We don't want you missing too."

Lily hastened to the window, the day darkening along with the mood of the house, both growing gloomier by the moment, and a few flakes of snow wafted from the sky. Not enough to cause alarm…for the moment.

Clasping her shawl close, she scurried to the study

where Asher sat, writing a list of possible hiding places. She leaned against the door frame, watching as he clutched his head in his hands and then raised it again, steepling fingers under his chin.

"Asher?"

A strained smile graced his lips. "Come sit by me, Lily."

Unusually, this study at Helmdon Court wasn't a deeply masculine place as Rosalind had made her mark with sofas and a delicate writing desk. Lily peered around for a chair, but he patted his thigh as he'd done in the woods.

She cautiously lowered herself onto his knees but was abruptly yanked back to sit deeply in his embrace, warmth engulfing her.

"That's better. Now look," he said, pointing to a well-drawn map with lots of neat red circles. "I know exactly where an enemy on the run would hide. I know where an injured soldier would shelter. But little people? I'm at a loss."

"I ran away from my husband once," she murmured, almost to herself.

"Oh, Lily. I had no idea it was so bad."

"No. But I was young. Eighteen. And he shouted at me for spilling soup down my gown at some important dinner. I felt such a disappointment to him."

"Where did you run to? And where would a child go? In winter? The night before Christmas Eve?"

"Well, I… I didn't go anywhere." Time-worn memories invaded Lily's mind.

Asher frowned. "What do you mean?"

"I… Who says Robert is running? I hid in the coal cellar. I just wanted somewhere to lick my wounds and…and for my husband to miss me. But I didn't run." She turned in his arms. "And I can't believe Robert would abandon little Alice either, not when he stole to feed her in Whitechapel."

"The house has been searched top to bottom."

"They searched for me all day too. But no one looked in the coal cellar."

Asher leaped up and she slid from his lap. "Lily, you are a genius."

THEY BOTH STOOD in the freezing cold, staring into the full, but Robert-less, coal shed. There were no cellars at Helmdon Court.

"It was a good idea, Lily."

"Bleugh. I suppose, but I was a young girl and boys are different. I'll go and fetch warm drinks for everybody." She reached up for a kiss and although his body fully reciprocated, his mind had wandered off.

"I'll be there soon," he called, watching until she entered the warm house.

With daylight rapidly fading, he scanned the yard. Lily was right: males thought differently. To begin with, Asher had found it difficult to put himself in the shoes of an eight-year-old boy – his own family had always told him he'd been born old, but now he remembered his siblings.

Frogs. Mud. Animals. Horses...

He headed to the stables, aware a search had already taken place, but people often overlooked the obvious – especially when in a distraught state.

Lucas's equine arrangement was a large affair – less draughty than the house – with huge stalls and rooms laid out to tack. Only a few boys milled about, as all the men were out combing the estate.

"Excuse me," he asked the nearest stablehand, a grubby lad, looking most disgruntled.

"Yea? Wot?" he said, scratching his arse – it seemed the stables were firmly under roguish Ryan's influence.

"Has everywhere been searched here?"

"Course."

"Hmm. The tack rooms?"

"Yep and under the saddles."

Asher surveyed for some moments before noticing a trapdoor in the ceiling. "What's up there?"

"Hayloft, but Charlie broke the bleedin' ladder yesterday so no one can get up. Can I go now? Got better fings to do."

He nodded, and the boy trundled off.

Analysing this lower floor of the stables, he could see no access to the trapdoor without use of a ladder. A rope was possible, he supposed, but it would require the lad to be an agile little monkey.

Asher wandered to the outside of the wooden building, keeping an eye on the roof levels as he walked along one side. A porch overhung the main entrance and above it… above it was a shuttered window.

But how in the hell would…

The stablehand and a companion reappeared, pushing a carriage out through the huge double doors before abandoning it.

"Excuse me?"

"Wot now?"

Did this lad not comprehend he was addressing a personal saviour of the Prince Regent and an overtly bosky duke? Obviously not as he gave a belligerent stare and chewed his fingernail.

"Was a carriage placed there earlier?"

"Course. We have to wash 'em all there. Gettin' a cleaning for church. That all? I'm off to the trough."

Asher nodded absently and approached the carriage, wondering whether he ought to call someone sprightlier for what he was about to do. He could be wrong, however, and it wouldn't do to raise hopes.

After pushing the new-looking carriage nearer the porch, he boarded the back plate and swung himself up to the leather-covered roof.

Reaching the actual porch proved more troublesome, the slope awkward, but he hauled himself onto it by his fingers.

Once there, he crawled along, feet slipping on the icy tiles. Heights didn't usually bother him, but he was promptly aware of his own mortality, the hard ground below and his easily breakable spine. He couldn't leave the widowed Lily a widow again. And he hadn't married her yet…

Finally, he made it to the shuttered window and pushed.

It didn't move.

Sitting himself in a comfortable but arse-freezing position, he bashed the corner with his elbow and felt the hinge give a little.

Another bash and his foot slipped but a gap opened.

A clout and the hinge gave way on one side.

"Wot on earth yer doing?" shouted the stablehand from below.

"Er." He whacked the rest of the shutter inwards with his fist. "Fixing Lord Helmdon's windows."

Mumbling about daft culls, the lad nodded and puttered off once more.

The hayloft was dark, dingy and exactly the type of

place that Lily had mentioned hiding in, but no young lad sat amidst the hay awaiting his arrival. Asher really didn't have time to piddle about, so grabbing hold of the pitchfork, he tentatively stabbed the loose hay.

"Ow! Ger off me, you addle-pated nodcock," a reedy voice yelped.

Did all little people have such disrespect for their elders?

"Robert?"

A head poked out of the hay, scowling and growling. "Go away."

"You do know that Rosalind, Lucas and all the men of Helmdon are searching for you?"

"So?"

Asher sighed. Recalcitrant boys really weren't his forte and he considered alerting the household, but faint light still etched the sky, so it could wait a few moments.

He scrutinised the small person. "Why are you hiding?"

"They don't want me. I'm gonna sit 'ere for a bit then make my way to London after Christmas."

"And leave Alice?"

The lad's eyes dropped. "When I've earned enough, I'll come back fer 'er."

"Lucas and Rosalind are fraught with worry."

"Dunno why." He picked at his moth-eaten jacket. "They only wanted Alice and they're sending me away. That other cull told me. I don't belong 'ere."

"That is not true. I had...words with Stretton. He lied to you. They wish for you to attend the local village school, that is all."

The lad's thin forehead creased. "Why'd he lie then?"

If Asher had a guinea for every time he'd heard that question... "Because *he's* the ignorant bastard, not you."

A half-smile curved Robert's lips.

"They are good people, your new parents."

A shrug. "They've never known 'ardship. Stuck in this cosy house with servants and the like."

Rolling his eyes, Asher sat beside him on a pile of sheaves. "Lucas was a…soldier. You must know that?"

"A fancy fribble major," the lad muttered.

"Fanc– How do you think he got those burns?"

Another shrug. "Dunno."

"Robert, he was captured whilst on reconnaissance in France." Asher debated the whys and wherefores of revealing this information, as he knew Lucas had intended to shield the lad from both his and Rosalind's pasts, but maybe Robert needed to know they had also suffered.

Hell, what a strenuous occupation parenthood must be – surely there were books of instruction?

"Reconni wot?"

"Spying." The boy's eyes widened. "That 'fancy fribble' as you termed him, fought in many skirmishes, was tortured for information which he never divulged and almost died when captured and his prison set afire. He's saved hundreds of lives in service to his country and climbed his way up the ranks to major, battle by bloody battle."

The lad's mouth dropped open.

"And if you want to talk of hardship, I suggest you speak with Rosalind, whose own kin treated her in such cruel ways you cannot begin to imagine."

Robert scrunched his face. "They didn't say nothin'. They don't act like that."

"Appearances can be deceptive." Asher paused, shifting on the scratchy hay. "When you look at me, what do you see?"

"Eh?"

"I mean, how do I appear to you?"

"Yer want me to be honest?"

"Please." Although he did wonder if this was such a good idea as the lad's critical eye ran over his black superfine coat, buckskins and polished top-boots. It lingered on his Indian silk handkerchief.

"Well, yer look a swishy cull, so yer well-breeched with a rum crib. Probably went to one of them dandy schools." The lad scratched his head. "Yers drink and wench and gamble all night then sleep all day."

If only, thought Asher…not the wenching obviously.

Robert picked at a length of hay and then chewed the end nonchalantly so Asher did likewise, watching as the lad suppressed a grin.

Yes, the yokel affectation was probably rather incongruous with his immaculate white cuffs and gold links.

"The Rainham family, of which I'm one," began Asher, twiddling with the stalk, "are traditionally valets, and I spent my childhood shining boots and starching neckcloths. Nowadays, I do indeed own a 'rum crib' and 'swishy' title, but I forged them for myself through sheer hard work and dedication. No 'dandy schools', I assure you."

The hay dropped from the lad's mouth.

"I also… I do know what it is to be…the odd one out. Amongst my own siblings, I felt as though I did not belong, but you do belong here, Robert. Always remember that you are very much wanted and loved in this house." The lad stared at his scruffy boots, but Asher knew he'd heard. "And that is one of the most precious things we can have. To love, to be loved – by friends, family…wife."

The lad looked up, hesitant, and Asher saw the child which Robert tried so very hard to hide. "Are you sure? I ain't nothin' but a ragamuffin."

"Only *you* see yourself as such. I see a brave, loyal lad who, against all the odds, protected and provided for his baby sister on the streets of London. A lad adapting to a new life. It will take time, yes, but no one here has anything but kindness and love in their hearts for you both. As we speak, Lucas is frantic, Rosalind is pacing the woods and Billy is searching the village." He placed a hand on his shoulder. "Do you like it here?"

"S'pose. Slow-worms and stuff."

Realising that was a positive declaration, Asher stood. "And your new parents?"

"S'pose." He sniffed. "They're nice to me and Alice."

Niceness, Asher knew, was a rare thing in Whitechapel, where dog eat dog wasn't just a proverb.

"Let's all celebrate this Christmas together then with Lucas, Rosalind, Alice and all of us who care about you."

Robert nodded, fingers knotting a stalk of straw. "Hmm, I'd like that."

"Good. Now, do you *s'pose* we could leave this rat-infested abode?"

"I don't wanna break my neck going through that window again. Can't you get a ladder?"

"No. Someone called Charlie broke it apparently."

"Those stable boys 'ave no manners," Robert said, stumbling to the window. "Let's find Lucas and Rosalind, and then do yer s'pose cook's got some gingerbread left?"

CHRISTMAS EVE, AND ALL WAS WELL

Feeling a dab melancholic, Lily watched the kindling struggle to light the huge trunk in the drawing room grate. A yule log that appeared large in the woods was simply immense once inside the house and she doubted it would burn out by Easter – even if they *could* light it.

Last night, after the busy events of the day, they had all gathered over roasted chestnuts and jugs of mulled wine. Asher had been toasted as the hero, but he'd hailed her clever thinking.

They'd exchanged lingering looks and sly touches all evening, the memory of their intimacy warming her. And then…

Well, she'd half expected him to come to her bedchamber. He hadn't.

She'd thought to see him over breakfast. He'd already partaken.

Mayhap they'd kiss under the mistletoe. He'd disappeared out.

Asking Lucas, he'd said Asher was busy.

Busy?

She had stared out at the snowy scene before her, wondering how one could keep so busy, given that three feet of snow had covered the land and kept the horses stabled.

Instead, she had spent a pleasant day with Rosalind and Alice but…

It was Christmastide and the man she loved was missing. And there was no doubt she loved him. Everything about him – from his probabilities to his strong hands, from his deep understanding of people's ways to his factual brain.

But today, in the cold light of snow, unease had assailed her.

This past sennight had been a culmination of her year's adventures, and deep inside her now sat a core of strength, where before there had been a bitterness.

She had rediscovered…Lily.

But she worried that a part of her might always adhere to propriety – years of submissive appeasement could not be so easily banished, and perhaps Asher would tire of her prim ways… She knew she still flapped her shawl too much.

"You've rearranged the whole battalion," Lucas bemoaned as Robert moved all the tin soldiers to the left flank. "Welly would decamp to his tent in fury."

Lily couldn't help a smile though, as she beheld Lucas, Robert and Sir John re-enacting the Battle of Roliça.

"Where were you stationed, then?" asked Robert avidly, and gazed wide-eyed as Lucas explained tactics and positioning.

Rosalind sat by the fire, humming and cradling little Alice, who seemed content to simply be cuddled. There was no doubt there would be trials ahead for Lucas and Rosalind with both children, but for now, on this Christmastide…all was well.

The other guests lounged contentedly, softly chatting or reading.

"Where's Jack?" Lily suddenly asked, realising he'd also been absent most of the day.

"Here I am, lovey," a jovial drawl called from the doorway. "Did you miss me?" He winked. "Now, everyone, into your cloaks and coats. Bring your muffs and womanly warm things. We are off out."

"Outside?" Lily squinted but only saw her reflection in the night-blackened glass of the window.

"Especially you, my fair Lily." Jack smiled and bustled men and boys into the hallway where servants held all manner of outdoor togs.

"Rosalind, do you know what is happening?" she asked as a maid adeptly slid a lilac cloak around Lily's shoulders.

"No and it's dreadfully annoying. I tried to coax information from Lucas with kisses but he…" Rosalind flushed. "Anyway, I *have* noticed the disappearance of my best candles and someone has been in the attic."

"How curious." Lily rescued her tasselled shawl from the side table and slipped it around her neck. A lady should never be seen without such an essential accompaniment.

Once they were all deemed suitably dressed, Jack threw open the main door and everyone peered out.

The snow had ceased falling at around midday and the landscape now glittered under a nearly full moon. No wind disturbed this pristine view; all rested in utter silence, a different form of silence – peculiar and divine.

Having trooped outside, their little group stopped as one to gasp.

"Cor!" said Robert and Billy together.

"Oh!" sighed Lily, Rosalind and the other ladies.

"Cheap," muttered Stretton.

Ahead, twisting left of the house, lay a path of lanterns. The snow had been beaten down to form a track and either side, guiding the way, was a raft of candlelight. A few trees similarly held lamps, the soft flames flickering on the crystal-laden branches. The damp dullness of winter had metamorphosed into a magical land of pure pearl.

"That truly is beautiful," murmured Rosalind. "But where is it headed? There's only the–"

"Ladies first," Jack declared, bowing. "May I have the pleasure of escorting you, Lily?"

"Thank you," she replied, laying her hand atop his, excitement pulsing in every nerve as the two of them led everyone down the winding path.

Asher had to be behind this. She'd been muddle-headed to fret while he had obviously been creating this enchanted land of light and ice.

They trod slowly, not just because the ground was slippery, but also to admire the small snow-hewn animals that sat along the way: a bear, a mouse, an owl and a funny butterfly which Jack informed her sternly was a moth – did she not notice the large head?

It was greatly cold tonight, their breaths panting white and noses numbing, but nevertheless the beauty of it all warmed their souls whilst they spoke in hushed murmurs. Plants bowed their heads as their procession passed, burdened by their new pristine white coats.

"Jack, doesn't this lead to…" They skirted the large oak, by which stood a strange turnip-shaped snow animal. "… the lower lake?"

In front lay a glistening sheet of ice. Tall candelabras

holding fat quivering candles were set upon the surface, and a table stood in the middle bearing champagne and glasses. Asher skated towards them, gliding on the frozen lake as though born to it, skimming like a swallow.

"Welcome, all, to my evening's entertainment. Skating shoes can be found on the benches to your left. Jack, if I could intervene to escort Lily."

Excited chatter arose as Billy and Robert wrestled to the seats, sliding over the icy ground.

"My pleasure, old boy. Good luck," Jack said, lifting a dark brow as he folded Lily's hand over Asher's arm and gave it a pat. "Rule twelve. Everyone loves surprises."

Lily yelped as they stepped forward. "Asher… I can't walk on the ice."

"'Tis fine, and I will assist." He led her onto the wintry expanse, her feet slipping for a moment, but Asher's strong arm held her tight and close.

"Hey," shouted Lucas. "What's the chance of this ice breaking under my weight?"

"As low as your wife not kissing you before the next call of owls," Asher lobbed back. "But no one need worry. The lake has been slowly freezing all week as it's undisturbed by running water. Perfect conditions so…all is well."

Lily was most impressed by his attention to detail, care and forethought, and wanted to throw her arms around him, but she was too scared of slipping.

"What happens if I fall?" she whispered.

"I will catch you, Lily." The low, rasped words stuttered her breath. He paused. "But if I don't, the best way to fall is on the arse. Less chance of breakages."

She batted his arm at his teasing, when all of a sudden yelling tore the night.

"No!" a lady shouted.

"Catherine, you will return with me to the house. I will not have you…huddling up with that lowly baronet on the ice," bellowed Stretton from the lake's edge whilst Catherine teetered on her skates with Sir John.

"No, brother. No more. This baronet has asked me to marry him and I have consented."

"You bloody won't!"

"I bloody will," Catherine roared, silencing the very air in her wake. "I love him."

"I only want what is best for you."

"No. That is a lie. You don't want to be alone with only your stupid title for company. But I want more. I want John."

Stretton's shoulders visibly sagged in the soft light. "Catherine, please…"

"I love you, brother, always. And you shall be a fine and devoted uncle to any children I am blessed with. You may tell them of our family's heroic deeds, and I shall love you for it, as will they. But I need you to let me go."

A pause, in which it seemed even the moon held its breath, but forthwith, Stretton's head slowly nodded. Catherine flew into his arms and hugged him soundly, before tottering back to Sir John, patiently waiting on the icy surface.

Jack approached Stretton with a large glass of champagne and a pair of skates, before placing a hand to the viscount's shoulder.

And on this Christmastide…all was well.

Twisting back to Asher's smile, Lily noticed a silk-covered chair had been placed under the boughs of a tree overhanging the lake, a table by the side holding two glasses of champagne.

"Oh, Asher. It is all too wondrous."

. . .

FEELING RATHER PLEASED with her reaction, Asher led his beloved to the chair and crouched by her. "You stir me to things I have hitherto never comprehended," he said, taking her left booted foot in hand.

"I worried today."

"What about?" he asked, slotting a skating shoe over the boot.

"Everything. You. Me. The future."

Kneeling, he handed her a glass of champagne. Perhaps he shouldn't have deserted her the day after they'd made love, but this idea had been a fine one, and he'd realised that to complete it would take all the daylight hours – even with Jack's help.

"I should have left you a note, Lily. I apologise but I am still learning about..." He dragged fingers through his hair, leaving frost in the strands. "Damn, I thought to begin with skating, but for the first time in my life, I find I have no...patience."

He smoothed her lilac skirts with a hand, his knee slowly freezing to the ice. Love had come late to his life, but never had anything been so worth waiting for. He could only hope she felt the same.

"For what?"

"To declare myself. My intentions. My...love."

"Ash–"

"No, not yet. Hear me. I know you desire and...like me, and I know 'tis too soon for you, but I do love you, Lily Mereworth, and I do not want only a Christmas dalliance. I am also aware that talk of marriage is too soon but that is what I would want to ask of you in time."

"Ash–"

"I will try not to work such long hours but occasionally it will happen. I am not even able to speak of my work some days, but please know I will never expect you to wait upon me. I want you to continue making yourself hideously rich. To beat me at cards. I want to come home and find you fast asleep, a scandalous novel in your hand."

"Ash–"

"I know you never wanted to marry again, but a year, Lily. I ask for one year – to court you, to love you, to listen to you. To learn about love together."

"Ash–"

"If you wish we can–"

LILY KISSED HIM, passionate and intense, grabbing his neck, the only way to halt his words. For once, he hadn't been listening to her, but she didn't care one whit. Asher would never object if she interrupted him, would never rebuke or belittle her.

A box caught her eye on the table, a small square box, and her heart flipped with excitement and trepidation.

"What's in there?"

"Ah. Hmm. I wanted to give you…something. A token of my intent and love. I would hope to replace it one day with a wedding ring, but for now…"

He handed over the velvet-swathed box and her hand trembled. Mr M had given her the hugest most garish diamond ring on the occasion of their betrothal and she'd hated it. That alone should have been warning enough.

With a creak, the lid hinged, and she had to tilt the box to view its contents. The moon bestowed a bluish glow tonight, spilling its radiance across the ice, but the candles shone amber, their flames glittering on the…

A slender gold ring sat upon a green silk cushion, the top of the band shaped, a bird rising.

Asher opened his mouth, but she forestalled him. "A phoenix! Oh, Asher, it's beautiful. Where in heaven's name did you get this?"

"Yes, well. That was actually my cufflinks. I visited the blacksmith today and with some monetary persuasion, he melted and hammered them into this ring. Then Jack, a surprisingly capable goldsmith, created the phoenix when the metal was still malleable. It was a little rushed and 'tis a bit lumpy but–"

"I love it, Asher." She threw her arms around his neck, breathed his citrus scent in the pure cold night. "I love you, Asher Rainham," she whispered in his ear.

"You do?" He frowned, pulling back, as though he hadn't considered that an option. "No. Are you sure?"

She laughed with delight. "Neither am I some young fizgig, and I *do* know I love you, but yes, I agree we've only had a short time together so a period of…adjustment, of courting, of loving would be perfect."

Asher was still shaking his head. "Are you sure though? There's only a one in a hundred chance of that happening. I calculated it myself on a blustery February night years ago."

Liberating the ring from its silk cushion, she placed it upon her finger. "I accept your troth, Asher Rainham. I love and adore you. I want to sleep naked with you and go on bold escapades – ice skating and new adventures."

"I love *you*, Lily. And I never want you to hide from me. You must tell me if I become distant or…odd. But never will I berate you for spilling soup. In fact, did I tell you I myself once tripped and spilled a whole decanter of port on Prinny's breeches?"

"Oh! What did he say?" she shrieked.

"He thanked me…after I told him it was poisoned."

Gracefully, Asher stood and held out his hands, smile broad and eyes twinkling as the frost shimmered about them.

Rosalind's laughter floated across the frozen lake, followed by a sly wink at them both, wicked and joyful, as she skated arm in arm with Lucas and Robert.

And on this Christmastide…all was well.

"Come then," Asher urged. "Come seduce a rogue and make your list complete."

"I hadn't realised you were also a rogue," she said, standing and taking those strong fingers to steady herself.

"Where you are concerned, the chances are I'll be the most incorrigible rogue you have ever encountered."

Asher skated backwards, holding her hands as she wobbled on the ice, steadying without force. Firm and accepting.

"Merry Christmas, my Lily."

Pure chilled air whipped her cheeks as she skated through the frosted night, laughing loud as Asher grinned and twirled her around, her tasselled shawl falling unheeded and abandoned to the ice.

Lily smiled. "Merry Christmas, my viscount."

The End

ALSO BY EMILY WINDSOR

RULES OF THE ROGUE SERIES

An Earl in Wolf's Clothing (Book 1)

From the hallowed halls of London's Almack's to the unkempt taverns of Drury Lane, from whispered words in glittering theatres to seductive encounters at Vauxhall Gardens – an earl must pursue his love.
A determined lady. An even more determined gentleman.
Let the pursuit begin...

Merry Christmas, my Viscount (Book 2)

Seduce a rogue? By Christmas Eve? What a troubling resolution for the most proper widow Mrs Lily Mereworth to be left with... How? And more importantly, who?
Ghost stories on a windy night, swordplay down the Great Portrait Gallery, a lady and a spymaster with no thought to love... Merry Christmas.

Let Sleeping Dukes Lie (Book 3)

"Strait-laced. Ruthless. Arrogant." – The Duke of Rakecombe has forever spurned love…and with good reason.
"Forthright. Impudent. Capricious saucebox." – The fiery Miss Aideen Quinlan refuses to be spurned, unable to erase the memory of the duke's vehement kiss…
An unlikely couple, an unquenchable passion.
Resistance is futile.

Marquess to a Flame (Book 4)

The Marquess of Winterbourne has long been guided by his *Rules of the Rogue*, but as spy for the Crown, his next mission will break every single one. Sent to the wilds of Cornwall to beguile secrets from a lady, the last thing this rogue expects is to unearth his own buried heart.

CAPTIVATING DEBUTANTES SERIES

Captivated by the Viscount

My Captive Earl

Her Noble Captive

ABOUT THE AUTHOR

Emily grew up in the north of England on a diet of historical romance and classical mythology.

Unfortunately, you couldn't study Georgian slang or the Regency London Season, so she did the next best thing and gained a degree in Classics and History instead. This 'led' to an eight year stint in engineering.

Having left city life, she now lives in a dilapidated farmhouse in the country where her days are spent writing, fixing the leaky roof, battling the endless vegetation and finding pictures of well-tied cravats.

Happy Reading,
Love,
Emily
x

facebook.com/AuthorEmilyWindsor
pinterest.com/EmilyWindsorBks
instagram.com/emilywindsorwritesregency
bookbub.com/authors/emily-windsor
goodreads.com/EmilyWindsor
amazon.com/author/emilywindsor

Made in United States
North Haven, CT
03 November 2021

10811385R00104